FROM THE
NANCY DREW FILES

THE CASE: Trace a blackmailer who has been preying on the employees of Cherbourg Industries.

CONTACT: Ashley Amberton, executive secretary at Cherbourg. She invites Nancy, Ned, and George to Montreal for a working holiday that proves to be extremely hazardous.

SUSPECTS: Jacques Olivier, the chauffeur who has more than one skeleton in his closet.

Lake Sinclair, a spoiled heiress who knows how to handle a gun.

Annette LeBeau, the TV newscaster in love with a dangerous man.

Dr. Emile Dandridge, the plastic surgeon who specializes in rich patients.

COMPLICATIONS: The blackmailer seems bent on testing Nancy to the breaking point—while George becomes a pawn in the game.

Books in THE NANCY DREW FILES® Series

Available from ARCHWAY paperbacks

THE NANCY DREW FILES™ CASE · 14

THIS SIDE OF EVIL

Carolyn Keene

AN ARCHWAY PAPERBACK
Published by POCKET BOOKS · NEW YORK

AN ARCHWAY PAPERBACK *Original*

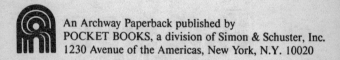

An Archway Paperback published by
POCKET BOOKS, a division of Simon & Schuster, Inc.
1230 Avenue of the Americas, New York, N.Y. 10020

ISBN: 0-671-64139-5

First Archway Paperback printing August 1987

10 9 8 7 6 5 4 3 2 1

NANCY DREW, AN ARCHWAY PAPERBACK and colophon are registered trademarks of Simon & Schuster, Inc.

THE NANCY DREW FILES is a trademark of Simon & Schuster, Inc.

Printed in the U.S.A.

IL 7+

Chapter

One

HEY, THIS ISN'T bad!" George Fayne exclaimed, looking around the nicely furnished apartment. "Not bad at all." She sat down on the floor in front of the stereo and began to fiddle with the knobs, tuning in a rock music station. "Look—there's even a VCR," she added. "If we get bored, we can always rent a movie."

Nancy Drew shrugged out of her black linen jacket and walked into the bedroom. Twin beds—room for both her and George. Ned Nickerson, Nancy's longtime boyfriend, could sleep on the living room sofa. "You're right," she agreed happily as she walked back into the living room. "Pretty neat. There's even a kitchen, so we can fix our own meals if we want to."

1

The apartment where they were to stay during their trip to Montreal, Canada, was small. It was on the sixth floor, though, and had a terrific view of the Saint Lawrence River. Nancy went to the window and looked out across the wide and gray river, which was crowded with ships. In the distance was a green island, dotted with oddly shaped buildings.

"That's Sainte-Hélène's Island," Ned said, coming up behind Nancy. "Where Expo Sixty-seven was held." He slipped his arm around Nancy's shoulders affectionately. "Maybe the world-famous detective could take a couple of hours off work to go sightseeing over there," he suggested.

Nancy returned his hug. "I hope so," she murmured, leaning against him. It was great to have Ned with her on this case. They'd been apart so often in the past few months that just being with him was like being on vacation —even if she *did* have to work. She thought back to her last case, *Wings of Fear,* which had taken Bess and her to Seattle, without Ned.

Nancy was in Montreal at the request of Ashley Amberton, executive secretary at Cherbourg Industries, to investigate a blackmailing operation within the company. It shouldn't be a big job, Ashley Amberton had told her, and it should leave some time for fun.

2

First, only George was going to accompany Nancy. But since Ned was on a break from Emerson College, he decided to come along as well to give Nancy a hand and—he said—to make sure she took some time off. This couldn't have made Nancy happier; it was spring, and spring in Montreal was beautiful and could be very romantic.

"Can you see Olympic Stadium?" George asked eagerly, coming to the window. She ran her fingers through her short, curly dark hair. "I can't wait to go running there."

"According to the map, the stadium's over that way." Nancy pointed upriver. "But I told you, George, I don't think there's a track in Olympic Stadium any longer. I've seen the Montreal Expos playing baseball on TV there, and I've never seen a track."

"There's got to be a track in there somewhere," George argued. "I mean, you don't just *destroy* a place like that." She laughed, her dark eyes sparkling. "The case of the missing track—I guess that's the first mystery we have to solve."

Nancy tossed her shoulder-length reddish gold hair. "That's *your* mystery," she told George, glancing at her watch. "I've got my own to solve. I'd better get going."

"Let me get my camera, and I'll walk with you part of the way," Ned said, picking up his tan windbreaker. "I'm going sightseeing."

* * *

Cherbourg Industries Ltd. occupied a tall chrome-and-glass building on Saint-Antoine Street in downtown Montreal, only a short walk from their apartment. Nancy took the elevator to Ashley Amberton's office on the fifteenth floor.

The office was wonderfully luxurious. Ms. Amberton must be a powerful person at Cherbourg Industries, Nancy thought, looking around. There was a balcony overlooking the river, velvety carpet on the floor, even a television set. A large telescope stood beside the window. Curious, Nancy bent over to peer through it. All she could see, though, was a large gray cargo ship with *Cherbourg* on the side. It was docked beside a mountain of crates on the wharf. Not a very inspiring view.

"And have you deduced the purpose of the telescope, Nancy Drew?" a woman asked coolly, her clipped speech emphasizing her air of efficient authority. The woman who had come into the room was tall and attractive in a tailored navy suit. Her black hair was pulled back into a French braid. Behind her black-rimmed glasses, her eyes were a pale, icy blue. She appeared to be around thirty.

Nancy straightened up. It was definitely the woman she had spoken to on the telephone, Ashley Amberton. "I suppose," Nancy said with a smile, "that you're checking out the

Cherbourg dockings."

"Exactly," Ms. Amberton said, sitting down in the black leather chair behind the massive desk. "I report the exact time of each ship's arrival directly to Mr. Cherbourg." She gave Nancy a measuring look. "I must say I'm surprised. From all I've read about you and your successes, I expected someone older."

Nancy grinned and took the chair in front of the desk. It was a comment she was used to hearing from her clients. "Youth doesn't necessarily mean inexperience, does it?" she replied meaningfully as she glanced around the elegant office. Ashley Amberton had obviously come a long way in a short time herself.

Ms. Amberton raised her thinly plucked eyebrows and gave a crisp nod. "I trust you're getting settled into the suite—you and your friends," she said. "You *did* bring your friends?"

Nancy nodded. "Ned's gone sightseeing, and George is trying to find out what they've done with the track in Olympic Stadium. She wants to run there."

"Good. I hope they find Montreal interesting for the short while you're here," Ms. Amberton said with a smile. "I mean, this should be a very easy case for a detective of your spectacular talents, Ms. Drew. I'm sure you'll wrap it up in no time."

"I hope so." Nancy took out her notebook.

"Why don't you tell me what you know about these blackmail schemes?"

"Very well. There are three cases, so far as I know," Ms. Amberton said, leaning back in her chair and removing her glasses. "The first involves my secretary, Monique Levere." She nodded toward a glass window. Nancy could see a secretary at work in the adjacent office. "Monique usually sits there, but she's at home with the flu today."

Nancy raised her pencil. "Would it be possible for me to interview her at home this afternoon?"

"Of course. I'll have Cynthia phone and tell her to expect you." Ms. Amberton picked up the telephone and spoke into it briefly. She sounded like someone who was used to being obeyed. In the outer office, the secretary hung up the phone and made a note on her pad.

"The second victim," Ms. Amberton continued, looking back at Nancy, "is one of our file clerks, Becky Evans. She works down at the end of the hall."

"And the third?"

"The third," Ms. Amberton said, "is Mr. Cherbourg's chauffeur, Jacques Olivier. I will arrange for you to interview both of them." She leaned forward and put her glasses back on, speaking in clipped syllables. "Even though this is a minor matter, Ms. Drew —nothing similar to the major crimes you are

6

used to dealing with—it must be cleared up immediately. Mr. Cherbourg is concerned about his employees. He's also worried that if people find out about this, it may reflect badly on the company. That's why we haven't called the police. It's a matter of the company's reputation."

"Of course," Nancy said soothingly. "I understand how important it is to get to the bottom of this quickly."

"And there's one more thing," Ms. Amberton added. "It's imperative that I know everything you discover, no matter how inconsequential, so that I can keep Mr. Cherbourg informed." She tapped her long, red-polished nails against the desk. "Is that clear?"

"Yes, of course," Nancy said with an inward sigh. It was always better to have free rein on a case, but she could understand that Ms. Amberton needed to be on top of things. "Now, can you tell me how you learned about the blackmail? Did the victims come and tell you about it voluntarily?" Nancy couldn't imagine wanting to tell her troubles to anyone with such cold eyes.

Ms. Amberton lifted her chin. "Of course not," she said. "I found a blackmail letter in Monique's desk drawer. When I confronted her with it, she told me that it was the third one she'd received."

"What about the other two?"

7

"A few days later I found Becky in tears in the washroom. When I pressed her, she confessed that she was also being threatened. I noticed Jacques acting strangely that same day, and he finally told me what was going on. Like Monique, they both received letters demanding money or their crimes would be revealed."

"How much were the payments?"

"Small amounts—fifty or a hundred dollars at a time. Of course, none of the victims have much money to spare."

Nancy looked at her. Ms. Amberton's stare was chilly. "And their crimes?"

The woman shrugged. "Petty, of course, little things out of their pasts that they don't want anyone to know about. A few years ago, Monique forged a check. She paid the money back, and the case was dismissed since it was her first offense. The file clerk stole some jewelry and was sent to jail for six months. And Jacques, the chauffeur—well, his crime was a good deal more serious. In fact, I haven't even told Mr. Cherbourg about it for fear that he would dismiss Jacques."

Nancy frowned. "What is it?"

"The man was involved with drugs, I'm afraid." Ms. Amberton tapped her fingers briskly on the desk. "Mr. Cherbourg is adamant about not employing drug users."

Nancy closed her notebook and stood up.

"I'd like to see both the file clerk and the chauffeur, please. And could you give me Monique Levere's home address?"

At that moment the door opened and a young woman stumbled in, looking dazed. It was the same woman who had been sitting at Monique's desk.

"Oh, Ms. Amberton," she gasped. "The most *awful* thing has happened!" She began to cry.

"Stop that sniffling, Cynthia," Ms. Amberton snapped. "And speak up. What is it?"

The young woman gulped back a sob. "It's Monique! She tried to commit suicide this morning, and her roommate, who answered the phone in her apartment, said she will probably die!"

9

Chapter

Two

MONIQUE HAD BEEN taken to the hospital in an ambulance, Nancy learned after Cynthia quieted a little. Ms. Amberton arranged for Mr. Cherbourg's chauffeur to drive Nancy to the hospital, and he was waiting downstairs when she hurried out.

"Bonjour, mademoiselle," he said, opening the door of the long black limousine.

"Bonjour," Nancy said, climbing into the backseat. She remembered that in Montreal most people spoke French. "Could I ask you a few questions?" she began as they rushed toward the hospital. In French, Nancy asked the chauffeur about the blackmail demands he had received, but he couldn't tell her much more than she already knew.

"Oui," he said. "There were letters, two of them. They wanted money, more money than I have."

"But you paid?" Nancy asked.

He nodded, looking straight ahead. "When Ms. Amberton found out that I was in trouble, she lent me the money. I cannot pay her back, but at least I am no longer afraid of losing my job because I cannot meet the demands of the blackmailer."

Nancy frowned. She'd almost rather risk the wrath of a blackmailer than borrow money from someone like Ashley Amberton. "Did you save the blackmail letters?"

He pulled some papers out of his uniform pocket and handed them to her. "Here they are," he said, with what sounded like relief. "I hope you catch this crook. It is a horrible thing to be blackmailed. I live in fear every day of losing my job."

"I understand," Nancy told him. "I can't promise you anything, but I'll do my best to get this straightened out as soon as possible."

She got out of the limousine in front of the hospital. Hurrying up the steps, she glanced quickly at the two letters the chauffeur had handed her. The message, typed in French, was identical in each one: "Put $2,000 in a red plastic bag and drop it into the trash can at Nelson's Column on Monday at noon. If you

11

don't, your employer will learn about the drugs."

Monique Levere was alive, Nancy discovered, but pale and groggy after her narrow escape from an overdose of sleeping pills. There was a frightened look in her eyes as she lay in the hospital bed.

Nancy introduced herself and asked Monique what had happened. In a small voice the young woman told Nancy that she'd been sick for a few days. She had taken a sleeping pill in the middle of the night, and the next thing she knew, she was in the emergency room having her stomach pumped.

"I told the police a million times that I took only one pill, to help me sleep," Monique said. "They don't believe me, though. They say I got sleepy and took the whole bottle by mistake —or that I tried to kill myself!"

"Did you keep the bottle beside your bed?" Nancy asked calmly.

Monique nodded, obviously fighting hysteria. "I think somebody put something into that pill! I think somebody tried to kill me!"

Nancy sat down beside the bed. "Can you think of a reason why someone might want to kill you?" she asked.

Monique shook her head. "Not unless it was the blackmailer." She gulped. "I can't pay any more. Maybe he got tired of waiting for me to pay and decided to kill me."

"How much have you paid altogether?" Nancy asked.

"Hundreds of dollars," Monique moaned. "Maybe as much as five hundred."

Nancy shook her head. Five hundred dollars was not that much, really. And there was no reason to believe the blackmailer would gain anything from Monique's death. "What did the letters say?"

"They all said the same thing: 'Put the money into a red plastic bag and throw it in the trash can at Nelson's Column. If you don't, your mother will find out that you are a forger and a thief.' It was so long ago," she added, "and in another city even. I never *dreamed* anyone would find out about it! I thought I was safe!"

"Why your mother?" Nancy probed.

Monique broke into tears. "My mother is old and sick. News like that could *kill* her!" She looked up imploringly, tears streaming down her face. "You've *got* to find the blackmailer, Ms. Drew! My mother's life depends on it, and so does mine!"

"Have you still got the letters?"

"They're at home." She turned her head away, sniffling loudly. "You can have them if you want."

13

"What about the bottle of sleeping pills?" Nancy stood up to go.

"The police took it, but I know it was empty." She turned back toward Nancy and smiled weakly. "If you see Ms. Amberton today, please tell her that I'll be back at work very soon. And thank her for coming to my apartment yesterday and bringing me flowers. They're beautiful."

I guess I'll have to revise my opinion of Ashley Amberton, Nancy thought as she left the room. Lending money to one of the blackmail victims, bringing flowers to a sick employee. Maybe she wasn't really as unfeeling as she appeared.

Nancy walked down the front stairs, biting her lip with a puzzled frown. It hardly seemed possible that a blackmailer—any blackmailer —would run the risk of discovery over such small amounts of money. And was it only hysteria, or did Monique have reason to believe that she had narrowly escaped being a *murder* victim?

The chauffeur was waiting outside the hospital to drive Nancy back to the Cherbourg Building. She was silent most of the way, thinking through what she had learned so far. Monique's story seemed convincing. Nancy was sure she honestly thought she hadn't taken

14

enough of the sedative to cause any harm. Had someone slipped something else into the bottle?

"I have one more question," she said, leaning forward to talk to the chauffeur as they wove through the heavy late-afternoon traffic on Université Avenue. "Do you have any idea how the blackmailer could have learned about your drug use?"

Jacques shook his head. "No," he replied, "but I did spend two years in prison, so I suppose it is a matter of public record." He hesitated, glancing nervously at Nancy. "I even changed my name from Xavier to Olivier on my application for this job—just to make sure my past was not found out. I don't know how the blackmailer has managed to trace me."

"*Merci*," Nancy replied. "Oh, and one more thing, Jacques. Please be careful."

"But why?"

"Because at least one person," Nancy said slowly, "believes that our blackmailer may also be trying his hand at murder."

In the lunchroom at the Cherbourg Building, Nancy met with the file clerk, Becky Evans. Becky was a nervous little blonde with large frightened eyes. She kept glancing over her shoulder to make sure nobody was listening.

15

"I've heard about Monique," Becky whispered. "Is—is she going to be all right?"

Nancy nodded. "She's still a little groggy, but she'll be fine in a day or two. I must tell you, though, that Monique suspects that the medication she took was poisoned," Nancy said, stirring her coffee.

Becky was staring at her, her eyes dark with fear. "Poison?" she whispered.

Nancy nodded. "There's no way to be sure, at least not yet. But you should be careful." She took out her notebook. "Now, what can you tell me about the blackmail letters you've received?"

"I've gotten three of them over the last six months," Becky said, swallowing hard. Reaching into her shoulder bag, she pulled out an unopened envelope. "And here's the fourth." She thrust it into Nancy's hands. "This was in my mailbox when I went home for lunch today."

Nancy examined it closely. It was a plain white envelope, postmarked in Montreal. "How do you know it's from the blackmailer?"

Becky pointed at the typed address. "Because it looks just like the others. It's addressed to Rebecca Veronica Evans, and I *never* use my full name. Besides, it doesn't have a return address. You open it. I just can't look."

16

Nancy opened the envelope and carefully unfolded the single sheet of paper. It was a blackmail letter all right, but it wasn't for Becky. It was for somebody named Annette LeBeau!

"Just a reminder that it's almost time for the third installment," the letter said. "So you can start getting the $20,000 together. If you don't pay, all your fans will know that you kept Dutch Medina out of jail, where he belongs."

Nancy quickly folded the letter. She hoped her face didn't betray her surprise as she turned back toward Becky. "I suppose you've kept the letters," she remarked in a deliberately casual voice.

The girl nodded. "I'll bring them in tomorrow and leave them with Ms. Amberton."

"One more question," Nancy said. "Do you have any idea how the blackmailer found out about the theft and the sentence you served?"

"I don't have a clue," she replied bitterly. "But I'll tell you one thing. This last letter —and Monique's poisoning—are the *last* straw. When this is over, I'm going to quit my job and get out of Montreal for good!"

After Becky had left, Nancy sat for a few moments, thinking. She had her first real lead now. The blackmailer had made a careless mistake in mixing up the letters. It proved

17

that Ashley Amberton had been right when she said there might be other victims. But who *was* Annette LeBeau, and how could she afford to hand over sixty thousand dollars? Nancy read the letter again. The blackmailer mentioned her *fans*. Was she a movie star?

On the way back to Ms. Amberton's office, Nancy looked at her watch. It was only four o'clock, plenty of time. She stopped at a pay phone and called the apartment. Ned answered.

"I hope you've had enough sightseeing," Nancy told him, "because there's work to be done. I need you to run over to the *Journal* morgue and find out everything you can about Annette LeBeau and Dutch Medina."

"No problem," Ned agreed. "Are you on to something already?"

"I think so. It looks like our blackmailer has expanded his territory," Nancy explained. "He might even be getting into murder. I'll tell you about it tonight."

"Speaking of tonight," Ned said, teasing her by speaking in an exaggerated French accent, "I've found a great little place for dinner—a *romantic* dinner just for two."

Nancy giggled. "Sounds terrific, Nickerson," she said. "But don't forget about George."

18

"Right," Ned said with a resigned sigh. "Dinner for three."

In Ms. Amberton's office, Nancy reported what she had learned from the blackmail victims.

"Do you think Monique really tried to kill herself?" Ashley Amberton asked.

Nancy shook her head. "You'd know that better than I would, but I'd say that her fear is genuine. She really thinks somebody tried to kill her. Of course, it is possible that she just got sleepy and forgot how many pills she'd taken."

Ms. Amberton sat down in her leather chair. "I don't like it," she said, tapping her red nails on the desk. "This is getting serious."

"There's more," Nancy went on. She opened her purse and took out the letter she had gotten from Becky. "Do you know somebody named Annette LeBeau?"

Taking the letter, Ms. Amberton scanned it quickly. Her face became clouded with concern. Then she picked up a remote control and snapped on the TV.

"This isn't small-time blackmail anymore," she said, flicking across the channels. "This is the big time." Just then the face of an attractive, vivacious blonde filled the screen. The camera zoomed back to show that the woman

19

was holding a microphone in her hand. With her was a man whom Nancy recognized as the prime minister of Canada.

"That," Ashley Amberton said, putting down the remote control, "is Annette Le-Beau!"

Chapter

Three

I THOUGHT THIS was going to be a quick, simple case," George said at dinner that night. Nancy had just told her and Ned about her afternoon's work. George stabbed a bite of Café Renoir's famous spinach salad. "And here we are, up to our eyebrows in crime already. Four blackmailings, one attempted murder——"

"Hey, not so fast," Nancy warned, finishing the last of her shrimp. George loved to solve mysteries almost as much as she did—the more the merrier. But it never hurt to be careful. "Let's not leap to any conclusions. We don't know for sure that somebody actually tried to kill Monique. *She* claims it's true, but it may not be."

"Yeah," Ned agreed in his usual, cautious

way. "Maybe she actually *was* sleepy and just lost count of her pills."

Nancy turned to Ned. "What'd you dig up at the *Journal* this afternoon?"

"'Dig up' is right," Ned said, pulling out a notebook. "It looks like there's plenty of dirt in this case." He tore out a couple of pages and handed them to Nancy. "Annette LeBeau, as you already know, is a prominent TV personality up here. Sort of a cross between a gossip columnist and an investigative reporter. She makes a lot of money finding out who's up to something dirty and then tattling on them."

George grinned. "Sounds to me like an ideal blackmail victim. Poetic justice, you might say."

"What about Dutch Medina?" Nancy asked.

"The plot thickens. Medina, it turns out, is a big-time mobster, a real creep. The police have been after him for years, but he's slick, and they've never been able to pin anything on him."

"According to the blackmail note," Nancy said thoughtfully, "Annette LeBeau kept Dutch Medina out of jail."

"So," Ned said, "things are getting a little more complicated. Looks like we've jumped from bargain-basement blackmail up to the real thing." He took a bite of his broiled fish. "I wonder what Annette LeBeau is like."

"Well, we'll know tomorrow," Nancy told them. "I've got an appointment with her at eleven—courtesy of our not-so-friendly client, Ashley Amberton."

"Why 'not-so-friendly'? What's she like?" George asked eagerly.

"Brisk and businesslike," Nancy replied. "If it weren't for the flowers she took to Monique and the money she's lent Jacques, I'd say she was as warm as an Arctic glacier. Now, who knows?" She grinned and pulled out the type-written blackmail notes she had collected. "How about an assignment for the two of you?"

"Sure," George agreed with a shrug. "It doesn't look like I'm going to get to run in Olympic Stadium, anyway. The track's there, but it turns out that it's covered with Astroturf most of the time. They only uncover it for track meets. So, what do you have in mind, Nancy?"

"Typing detail," Nancy said, spreading the notes on the table in front of them.

"Oh, I get it." Ned picked up one of the notes and studied it. "You want us to check out the typewriters and letter-quality printers at Cherbourg Industries, to see if the black-mail notes were typed there."

"You got it," Nancy replied. "I'd say that these notes were all typed on a typewriter rather than done on a word processor. Anyway, it's possible that the blackmailer is connected with Cherbourg since three of the victims are company employees. We need samples from all the machines in the building —and that's going to take quite a while. You'd better polish up your typing skills."

"'Now is the time for all good men to come to the aid of their party,'" Ned murmured, flexing his fingers.

George gave Ned a disdainful glance and laughed. "Speaking of parties," she said, leaning toward Nancy and Ned, "how about trying out that club down the street? Chez Soda, it's called."

"Sounds like a winner to me," Ned said enthusiastically. He carefully refolded the notes and put them in his pocket. "Especially if there's dancing," he added. "Maybe I'll even get to put my arms around my favorite girl for a while." Ned flashed Nancy a grin.

"Sure," she said a little absently. She was already preoccupied with thoughts of her interview with Annette LeBeau the next morning. How would Annette feel, being the target of somebody else's questions for a change?

But after an hour at Chez Soda, Ned's arms tight around her and his lips against her cheek, Nancy had nearly forgotten Annette—and the case, too. And George had discovered that she could get along fine in Montreal without speaking French.

"All I have to know how to say is *oui*," she said when she got back to the table after a slow dance with a cute French guy.

Nancy shook her head, laughing. "Didn't anybody ever tell you that saying *oui* too much could get you into trouble?"

George flushed. "Yes, *Mom*," she said teasingly.

Chuckling, Ned reached out to squeeze Nancy's hand. "How about another dance?"

And Nancy was delighted to say, *"Oui."*

At the television studio the next day, Nancy met Annette LeBeau. The newswoman was in her dressing room, getting ready to film an interview with a suburban chief of police on the problem of crime in his area. She was just putting the final touches on her make-up.

"So, you're Nancy Drew," she said, turning away from the mirror to look at Nancy curiously. "I've heard about you. You're supposed to be some sort of hotshot supersleuth, aren't you?"

Nancy smiled. "I've had a few successes," she said modestly.

Annette turned back to the mirror and began to brush on mascara with expert strokes. "So, what do you want with me?" she asked. "Ashley Amberton said it was urgent."

"It is," Nancy said. She sat down at the

makeup table so she could see Annette's face in the mirror. "It's about blackmail."

Annette's hand jerked, and she smudged the black mascara on her cheek. But she recovered immediately. "Blackmail?" she asked in an innocent voice as she wiped away the smear. "I don't know what you're talking about."

"Oh, I think you do," Nancy replied casually. "I'm talking about you and Dutch Medina."

Annette swiveled her chair around, her eyes narrowed. "Listen," she hissed, "if you think you can come in here and threaten me—"

"I'm not threatening you," Nancy assured her. "I want to help, if I can." She took out the letter Becky Evans had given her. "I think this was meant for you."

Annette paled under her makeup as she read the letter. "How did you get this?"

"The blackmailer sent it to one of his other victims by mistake," Nancy said. She leaned forward. "How did you help Dutch Medina?"

Annette's face became a mask, with her mouth pressed into a tight line. "I don't have to tell you anything," she said in a hard voice.

Nancy stood up. "No," she replied pleasantly. "You don't have to say a word to me." She picked up her blazer, which she had put on the back of her chair. "You can go on making blackmail payments until the money runs out. Or you can go to the police and tell them—"

"But I can't," Annette burst out. Her composure was beginning to unravel. "I *can't* go to the police! If I did, everyone would find out that I was involved with Medina—that I faked his alibi!"

"So that's what the blackmailer meant when he said that you kept Medina out of jail?"

The woman slumped in her chair. "It was a long time ago, more than ten years. The prosecutor couldn't convict him because I swore that Dutch and I were together when a shooting occurred. I was such a fool! I was so sure he was innocent!"

"And now you can't afford to have people know about this," Nancy went on.

Annette bit her lip. "It would mean the end of my career." She turned to Nancy, her eyes pleading. "Listen, Nancy Drew, you've *got* to catch this blackmailer. He's making my life absolutely miserable—and not just *my* life, either!"

Nancy looked at her. "You know about other victims?" Of course! Annette had probably gotten Becky Evans's blackmail letter.

But she hadn't. Instead Annette explained, "Her name is Lake Sinclair. She was involved in a hit-and-run accident a year or so ago. She's been paying the bills for the victim's plastic surgery, not to mention whatever it cost to fix her own fancy yellow Mercedes. And now she's paying a blackmailer, too."

"How'd you find out about this?" Nancy asked.

"A few days ago Lake tried to sell me a piece of her family jewelry. I asked her what was going on, and she broke down and told me why she had to have the money." Annette shivered nervously. "I assumed that we were dealing with the same blackmailer, but maybe we're not. It could be someone else."

"There's no way of knowing until I check it out," Nancy said. She stood up. "Thanks for being straight with me, Ms. LeBeau. I hope we can get to the bottom of this quickly."

"Curiouser and curiouser," George said. The girls were in their bedroom at the apartment. George pulled her red lamb's wool sweater over her head and threw it on the bed. Then she stepped out of her black jeans. "*Another* blackmail victim?" She counted on her fingers. "That makes five, doesn't it?"

Nancy nodded. "Our blackmailer's been busy. No wonder he's making mistakes—like sending his demands to the wrong person." She scratched her head. "And I wonder what became of Becky Evans's letter. I thought maybe it would turn up in Annette LeBeau's mail, but so far it hasn't."

"I think this guy needs a computer," George said. "Might help him keep his victims straight." She pulled on her bathrobe.

"No kidding." Nancy took off her khaki-colored corduroy blazer and hung it up in the closet. "So how did you and Ned do today?" she asked, slipping off her loafers. She wriggled her toes. "Any luck with the typewriters?"

George went over to the dresser and took the blackmail notes out of her purse, handing them to Nancy. "I don't think so. It doesn't look like these were typed at Cherbourg Industries."

"Of course," Nancy said thoughtfully, "the blackmailer could still work there and have typed these at home." She pulled out the notes and began to examine them with the small magnifying glass she always carried in her purse. Shaking her head, she looked up. "I don't see anything special. Oh, by the way, where'd Ned go?"

Before George could answer, a knock interrupted them. George hurried into the living room to answer the door.

"Who is it?" Nancy asked.

"Just the bellman from downstairs," George called back. "He brought the newspaper up." She came back into the bedroom, unfolding it. Her face went suddenly white.

"Nancy," she gasped. "Look!"

Nancy looked at the paper in George's hands. Across the front page, in big black letters, the headline screamed "NANCY DREW DIES IN MONTREAL!"

Chapter

Four

NANCY DROPPED HER magnifying glass and snatched the paper away from George. She looked at it closely. "Look, George," she said, pointing, "the letters are all pasted up. And my picture has been cut out of another newspaper."

"Really slick," George said sarcastically, staring at the paper. "Whoever did this is so creative."

"Yeah," Nancy said, biting her lip. "And evil, too." She picked up the phone from the bedside table.

"Who are you calling?" George asked.

"The bellman," Nancy replied. "I want to find out how he got this paper."

The bellman couldn't tell Nancy anything specific. He said he'd found the paper downstairs, on the desk just inside the door of the apartment building. Somebody must have put it there when he was away. The room number was scrawled on it, so he'd brought it upstairs immediately.

"No leads there," Nancy said with a sigh, hanging up. "The street door is only locked at night. Anybody could have walked in and left it."

Just then Ned came home. He popped his head into the bedroom. "What's going on?"

Without a word, Nancy handed him the paper.

"Uh-oh," he said, taking it from her.

"'Uh-oh' is right," Nancy agreed soberly. "Looks like we've spooked our blackmailer."

Ned sat down on the bed, staring at the paper. "Where'd this picture come from, Nan? I don't recognize it."

Nancy frowned. "I've been trying to remember. It could give us a clue about who's behind all this."

Ned looked at Nancy. "Well, no matter who the blackmailer is, this case is getting serious. We're not dealing with somebody who's just shooting off interoffice memos for spare change. This is a *death* threat."

George frowned. "I wonder how many people—besides Ms. Amberton, that is—know that we're staying in this apartment."

"That's a good question," Nancy said grimly. "I'll ask Ashley Amberton tomorrow."

"Correction," Ned said. "*We'll* ask Ashley Amberton. I don't think you ought to work alone on this one, Nan." He reached for her hand. "Two will be safer than one."

George gave them a quick glance and picked up her cosmetic case. "Well, if you *two* don't mind," she informed them lightly, "I've got a date tonight—for a *French* lesson." She tossed her head and smiled devilishly. "I'm going to learn to say more than just *oui*." She disappeared into the bathroom, humming to herself.

Nancy sighed. It didn't take a detective to see that George had found a new friend—a very cute, very *male* friend. Who was this guy?

Ned squeezed her hand. "I'm ready for a romantic evening with my favorite girl. Want to try that Chinese restaurant we saw? Maybe go dancing again later?"

Nancy threw a questioning look in the direction of the bathroom. She hadn't seen George acting so crazy in months.

"Nickerson calling Drew," Ned said, into a pretend microphone. "How about a date tonight?"

"Affirmative," Nancy said, turning back to Ned. George would tell her everything later —if there was anything to tell, that is.

* * *

"I suppose anyone could've known where you're staying," Ashley Amberton said the following morning. "Everyone here at Cherbourg has access to the company apartment; all they have to do is reserve it."

"Who handles that?" Ned asked.

"A secretary down the hall."

"We'd like to speak to her, please," Nancy said.

The secretary showed Nancy and Ned the schedule of bookings for the apartment. Usually, they learned, the book hung on the wall beside the door. After Nancy questioned the secretary, it was clear that Ms. Amberton was right—anyone could have looked at the schedule.

Back in Ms. Amberton's office, Nancy shook her head. "No leads in that direction," she said.

"I'm becoming quite concerned." Ashley Amberton went to the balcony door to look out across the river. "This thing seems to be getting bigger every day. First that business with Monique, now the threat against your life." She threw Nancy a troubled glance. "Where is it going to end?"

"Do you know somebody named Lake Sinclair?" Nancy asked.

Ms. Amberton turned around sharply, surprise written across her face. "Lake Sinclair? Why, of course I know her. Her father is one of

Mr. Cherbourg's closest friends." She studied Nancy, her brows drawn together in confusion. "Why do you ask?"

"Because," Nancy said, "it looks like she might be another one of our blackmailer's victims."

"Lake?" Ms. Amberton exclaimed. "How did you find *that* out?"

Nancy told her what she had learned from Annette LeBeau.

"A hit-and-run?" Ms. Amberton dropped heavily into her desk chair. "You can't be serious. Lake's always been a little on the wild side, but she'd never do anything like that!"

"Maybe not," Nancy replied, "but we can't be sure about that, can we? And I have to follow every single lead, no matter where it takes me."

The woman nodded, watching Nancy with a look of grudging respect. "I see," she said softly, "that you are a *very* professional detective, Nancy Drew." She reached for the phone. "I'll set up a meeting with Lake."

Lake Sinclair's condominium, Nancy learned from Ms. Amberton, was located in a restored section of Old Montreal, near the wharves.

"You know what we could do?" Ned asked later that morning as they left the Cherbourg

Building. "We could get a calèche—you know, a horsedrawn carriage—and ride in style. But only if you'll promise not to say one word about business while we're on the way!"

"Oh, Ned, it sounds so romantic!" Nancy cried. "But what about George?" She pushed up the sleeves of her royal blue cotton sweater. "Shouldn't we call the apartment to see if she's back from her jogging? Maybe she'd like to go, too."

"Sure, but I think she has a date," he said. Ned reached in his pocket and pulled out a handful of Canadian coins. "Need change?"

"Yes," Nancy said and grinned. "Thank you."

Nancy let the phone ring a dozen times, but George didn't answer. "I guess she did go out," she said regretfully, hanging up the phone.

"So what do you say about that carriage ride?" Ned asked.

"What are we waiting for?" Nancy answered with a happy smile.

They walked over to the plaza, where Ned hailed a shiny black calèche, which was pulled by a large gray horse. Nancy climbed in, and just as Ned was about to get in beside her, he held up his hand. Asking the driver to wait for a minute, he disappeared in the direction of a flower stand. When he came back, he was carrying a tiny bouquet of violets and lilies of the valley. He handed them to Nancy with a grand flourish.

"Oh, Ned," she said, touched. "How sweet!" She held the violets against her blue sweater. They looked even more fragile and exotic against the bold color of her top.

"It wouldn't be a spring day in Montreal without flowers," Ned said, climbing in beside her.

Nancy leaned back in the seat, breathing in the rich fragrance of the flowers. The bright spring sunshine warmed her as the horse pulled the calèche away from the curb.

"This *was* a great idea," she said. Ned was right—for the next few minutes, Nancy would forget all about the case and just enjoy the Montreal sunshine and Ned there beside her.

Ned pulled his guidebook out of his pocket and looked through it. "Here on the left, ladies and gentlemen," he intoned, glancing up, "is the famous Nelson Column, dedicated to the British commander who—"

Nancy sat straight up. "The Nelson what?"

"The Nelson Column. Right over there."

Nancy looked where Ned was pointing. At one end of the open square stood a tall stone column with a statue on the top. "That's the place!" Nancy exclaimed.

"Hey, you're right!" Ned said. "The place our blackmail victims leave their payoffs!"

Nancy stared at the column. There was a trash can a few yards from it, probably the very one where the victims made their drops.

She thought for a moment. "You know, Ned," she said, "maybe the quickest way to wrap up this case would be to wait until there's another letter. Then stake out the drop and wait for the blackmailer to—"

Ned began to laugh. "Do you realize what we're doing?" he asked.

Guiltily, Nancy nodded. "Yes," she said with a sigh. "We're talking business again."

Ned squeezed her hand. "I understand," he said softly. "It's just so much a part of you that you can't really put it out of your mind, can you?"

Nancy shook her head. "Yes, I can," she said stubbornly. "Starting right now!"

After a while the calèche turned down a side street, the horse's hooves *clip-clopping* steadily on the pavement. The brick and fieldstone houses and small shops were built close to the street. They had steeply pitched copper roofs with dormer windows and brightly colored shutters. Some of the buildings also had wrought-iron balconies, and every now and then Nancy glimpsed a shaded courtyard, hidden between buildings. There were old-fashioned street lamps on every corner and pots of flowers beside the doorways.

Nancy sighed. "It looks just the way it must have looked a hundred years ago."

"Yeah," Ned replied as a car zipped around them. "If you ignore the cars." He slipped his arm around Nancy, and she dropped her head against his shoulder. "Hey," he said, nudging her. "There's Notre Dame. Isn't it beautiful?"

She turned and saw the pretty stone church with its central spire and two side pinnacles in front of them. And then she imagined her wedding day in a church just like that. What would her dress look like, and what would Ned—

"Hey, Drew," Ned said, "you got something on your mind?"

Nancy blushed. "Not at all, Nickerson," she said, smiling. "Not at all."

Ned's arm tightened around her and he bent toward her, his lips close to hers. "Nancy," he said softly, "I—"

Just at that moment, a car careened recklessly around them, grazing the wheel of the calèche. The frightened horse neighed, rearing up on his hind legs as the driver fought to control him. The horse raced off at breakneck speed, the carriage bouncing down a narrow cobblestone alley and around a corner, where its wheels ran up over the high curb. The carriage began to tilt dangerously.

"Hang on, Nancy!" Ned cried, holding her tight. "We're going over!"

Chapter

Five

THE BOUNCING CALÈCHE teetered on two wheels as the driver yanked desperately on the reins, pulling with all his strength and shouting, "Whoa! Whoa!" Nancy found herself thrown into one corner, with Ned's arms tight around her. She held her breath as the carriage rocketed over the curb and into the crowded street. But it stayed upright! After a moment the driver managed to bring the terrified horse under control. Amazingly no pedestrians had been injured.

"Are you okay?" Ned asked breathlessly when they finally came to a stop.

"I—I guess so," Nancy answered, her voice shaky as she tried to sit up straight. She rubbed her throbbing temple where she had bumped it.

Ned climbed out of the carriage and turned back to help Nancy down. She got out and began to dust herself off.

"Monsieur, mademoiselle, a thousand pardons! Please don't go!" the driver cried, climbing down from his perch. "My horse was frightened by the car, that's all."

Nancy nodded. "I know," she said, rubbing her head. "But I think I've had enough of calèches for one day." She reached into the carriage to pick up her flowers, and looked at Ned. "How about if we walk the rest of the way?"

"Good idea," Ned said. He tried to pay the driver, but his money was refused.

Lake Sinclair lived in one of the restored brick-and-stone buildings on Saint-Denis Street. On the outside the building looked as if it were untouched by modern technology. It appeared hundreds of years old, with its quaint iron railings and gray-green slate roof. Even the parking area had been cleverly disguised to look like an old brick courtyard.

But inside, Lake Sinclair's house was ultramodern, filled with sophisticated contemporary furniture and a few pieces of exceptional art. Lake herself was a beautiful young woman, only a few years older than Nancy. She was dressed in a chic white jogging suit. Her bright auburn hair had curled in damp tendrils around her face, which was flushed with color.

"You'll have to forgive me," she said, tossing her long hair carelessly. "I've just gotten back from a run in the stadium, and I haven't had time to change." She led them down a softly lit hallway. Off to one side, Nancy could see what looked like an athletic training room. It was full of exercise machines and weights. George would love this, Nancy thought.

"In the stadium?" Nancy asked eagerly. "My friend George is dying for a chance to run in Olympic Stadium, but we've been told it's closed to the public."

"I'm sure my dad would be glad to arrange something," Lake replied, showing them into the living room. She sank down onto the plush sofa and a white angora cat jumped up on her lap, purring loudly. "He's on the board of directors at the stadium."

"That would be great," Nancy said as she and Ned took the chairs opposite the sofa. "George will be delighted."

Lake looked at Nancy. "Ashley said that you're a private detective, and she asked me to—to cooperate with you, whatever that means." She hesitated, her eyes flickering from Nancy to Ned. "What can I do for you?"

Nancy leaned forward. Sometimes it was better to start out with small talk. In this case, though, she had the feeling that she would get more out of Lake if she took the direct approach.

"You can tell us about the blackmail demands you've been getting," Nancy said.

Lake's face paled suddenly. "Blackmail?" Her voice cracked. "I don't know anything about blackmail."

"We think you do," Ned replied sternly. "We think you know a great deal about it."

Lake took a deep breath. "And what makes you so sure of that?" she asked in a challenging voice. Her eyes darted from one to the other.

"I talked with Annette LeBeau yesterday," Nancy replied. "She told me that you offered to sell her some of your family's jewelry. She also told me why."

Lake gasped, her fingers tightening in the fur of the angora cat.

Giving her a direct look, Nancy explained, "I was asked to come to Montreal to break up a blackmailing scheme that appears to be centered at Cherbourg Industries. We know of four victims already. The same person could be blackmailing you. We'll have an even better chance of finding out who it is if you'll help us."

Lake looked at Nancy for a minute, her mouth tight. Then her lips began to tremble and tears gathered in her eyes, and her cat ran and hid under the sofa.

"It's not just the blackmail that's been tearing me apart," she whispered, her voice breaking. "It's knowing what I did to that poor little girl. Every night I dream about it— about the awful crash and the blood." She buried her face in her hands and began to sob.

"The girl you hit with your car—your yellow Mercedes?" Nancy asked softly.

Lake nodded. She looked up, her eyes filled with tears. "It was dark and rainy, and I was driving very fast. The child ran out in front of me and I hit her."

"You didn't stop, did you?" Nancy said.

Wordlessly Lake shook her head. After a moment she said in a shaky voice, "The next day I called the hospital, pretending to be a friend. I found out who she was. Then I promised her parents I would pay all of the hospital bills and find her the best plastic surgeon in the city, if only they wouldn't tell the police who had done it. It cost a fortune, but I *had* to do it."

"But why?" Ned asked. "If she ran out in front of you, it wasn't your fault."

"Maybe not." Lake bit her lip so savagely that it started bleeding. "But I couldn't take that chance. If my father ever found out what happened, he would have taken away my allowance, my car." She turned to look at the room around them. "I would have lost this house, and all my beautiful things."

"But now you're about to lose everything to a blackmailer," Nancy said.

Lake sighed and pointed to an empty spot on the wall. "The painting that was hanging there was my favorite. I sold it last month for nearly fifty thousand dollars. And every penny went to the blackmailer. I've sold nearly all the jewelry I inherited from my grandmother. There isn't much left." She shrugged sadly.

"How does the blackmailer contact you?" Nancy asked.

"Letters," Lake said. "Then I put the money —usually ten thousand at a time—in a red plastic sack and drop it in the trash can beside Nelson's Column." She laughed shortly. "I suppose the blackmailer hangs around and watches, then picks it up after I've gone. Pretty expensive trash."

Nancy flashed a look at Ned. It was the same modus operandi, or mode of operation. It must be the same blackmailer! Ned nodded. "Who could have found out about the accident?" he asked Lake.

She shrugged. "Somebody at the hospital, I guess. I went to visit the girl there once. I didn't give my name, though, and I wore a scarf and an old coat so I couldn't be recognized.

"You said something about plastic surgery," Nancy observed, taking out her notebook.

"Are you paying the bills for the girl's surgery by check?"

Frowning, she said, "Of course. But Emile Dandridge is the best plastic surgeon in the city," she tried to explain. "I mean, he does cosmetic surgery, and lots of his patients don't want anybody to know about their tucks and lifts. His work is always *very* confidential. I can't imagine that anybody in his office could be a blackmailer."

"Well, *somebody* is," Nancy said pointedly. She wrote down Emile Dandridge's name and the address and phone number that Lake gave her. Then Lake went upstairs and brought down the blackmail letters, all carefully locked in a heavy metal box. Nancy scanned them quickly. She couldn't be sure without a closer examination, but they looked exactly like the others.

"I—I hope you can find out who's doing this and make him stop," Lake said. The cat came out from under the sofa and rubbed against her. She picked it up, burying her face in its soft fur. "I don't know how much longer I can go on this way."

Outside, Nancy and Ned hailed a cab and went back to the apartment. On the coffee table there was a scrawled note from George. "Gone for a ride with Pierre," it read. "Back at six."

"Pierre?" Nancy said, reading the note. "I guess he's the guy she met at Chez Soda."

"I suppose," Ned answered. He pulled the drapes open, and the late-afternoon sunlight flooded the living room.

Ned ran his fingers through his brown hair. "So, what's next?"

"How about if I make us some lemonade? I saw a mix in the cupboard in the kitchen."

"Sounds good," Ned agreed. He followed her into the kitchen and leaned against the door jamb, watching as she took down a pitcher and some cups. The kitchen looked almost new. Obviously, it hadn't been used very much.

"Let's see," she said, going over to the cabinet above the stove. "I think the mix was up here." She reached up over her head and tugged on the door.

"That's funny," she said. "I don't remember this cabinet being so hard to open."

She yanked again, and the door popped open. As Nancy struggled to keep her balance, she saw the metal Thermos that was perched on the very edge of the top begin to wobble. It was going to fall! Instinctively, Nancy put up a hand to shield her face, but she was too late. A dense white mist poured out of the Thermos. Whatever it was, it was steaming—and it was about to splash into her eyes!

Chapter

Six

WHAM! NANCY WAS hit. Ned had just knocked her out of the way of the steaming waterfall. The two of them landed on the floor next to the sink, and a moment later Nancy sat up, dazed. For a second she just sat still with Ned's arms wrapped protectively around her. She sank back against him as she watched the cloud of white vapor spilling from the stove onto the floor.

"Let's get out of here, Ned!" she cried, struggling to her feet. "Somebody rigged that cannister to fall when the door was opened. It could be poisonous!"

"Wait," Ned said calmly. "If somebody had wanted to poison us, he wouldn't have tried anything so complicated, or so messy." He shook his head, frowning. "No, this isn't poison."

"Then what is it?" Nancy asked. She stepped closer and looked at the puddle on the floor. It was already beginning to evaporate into clouds of steam. "It's steaming—is it hot?"

Ned disappeared into the living room. In a minute he came back with a floppy green leaf from a philodendron plant. Carefully he dipped the leaf into what was left of the puddle. When he pulled it out seconds later, it was covered with frost. And when he tapped it gently on the counter, it shattered into a dozen pieces of what looked like green ice!

"It's frozen!" Nancy exclaimed. She looked at Ned. "Wow! Where did you learn that trick?"

"Freshman chemistry," Ned replied, staring at the shattered leaf. "This stuff is probably some sort of a liquefied gas."

"But what kind?" Nancy asked.

"I don't know—yet," Ned said thoughtfully. "Actually, the possibilities are pretty limited. When most substances get this cold, they freeze solid."

"Like the leaf," Nancy said.

"Yeah. Like the leaf." Ned leaned closer. "Let's see. There's no color—that white steam is probably just the water vapor in the air freezing when it comes in contact with the gas."

Nancy sniffed. "I don't smell anything, either."

"Neither do I," Ned said, reaching for the box of matches on the stove. "I wonder if it burns."

Nancy grabbed his arm. "Are you crazy, Nickerson? The air is filled with the stuff. If it's flammable, this place could go up like a box of fireworks!"

"My bet is that it isn't," Ned argued. "But you're right. We need to be on the safe side." He got out a long-handled spoon and carefully scooped up a spoonful of the fuming liquid. Carrying the spoon into the other room, he touched a match to it. The flame died immediately. "My bet is that this stuff is liquid nitrogen—it doesn't burn."

"Okay, enough with the chemistry lesson," Nancy said impatiently. "What would have happened if this stuff had gotten in my eyes a few minutes ago?"

Ned looked at her seriously. "You'd probably be blind," he said. "And you'd need plastic surgery. You'd be badly scarred."

Nancy shuddered, thinking how narrowly she had escaped. If it hadn't been for Ned's quick action . . .

"Who would have access to liquid nitrogen?" she asked, pushing the thought of danger away. "It's not the kind of stuff you'd find on the drugstore shelf, is it?"

Ned shook his head. "Only chemists, physicists, people who work with low-temperature materials—they're the ones who'd be likely to have it," he said. "Like astronomers making artificial comets, or doctors and medical technicians who freeze tissue for microscopic slides, or manufacturers—"

"Doctors!" Nancy interrupted him excitedly. "Plastic surgery! Emile Dandridge is a plastic surgeon!"

"Hey, yeah," Ned said. "In fact, up until a few years ago, doctors used liquid nitrogen to burn off warts."

"Then he—or somebody in his office —could have access to it," Nancy pointed out thoughtfully. "And the same person could have known about Lake Sinclair making those payments for the girl!" She looked at Ned. "Let's go see how the booby trap was set up. Maybe that'll give us a clue."

In the kitchen the puddles of liquid nitrogen were almost completely gone. It had evaporated into the air. Above the stove, the cabinet door was still open. Lying on the top shelf was a large metal Thermos—empty. The Thermos stopper hung suspended from a short string that was fastened to the inside of the cabinet door with a thumbtack.

Nancy climbed up on a chair so she could see onto the top shelf. "There's a short loop of string around the bottom of the Thermos," she reported to Ned. "And the loop is tacked to the shelf. When I opened the cabinet door, the string on the lid pulled the stopper out while the loop around the bottom held the Thermos in place. That's why it tipped over, but didn't fall."

"Pretty ingenious," Ned agreed. "He used the Thermos to make sure that the stuff stayed cold until the stopper was pulled out."

"Yeah," Nancy replied, climbing down and brushing off her hands. "The evidence goes up in smoke, and all we're left with is an empty Thermos and a couple of pieces of string."

"And, someone hoped, a blind detective," Ned reminded her. Tenderly, he put his arms around Nancy. "I'm so glad nothing happened," he whispered. He touched Nancy's cheek. "I like your face just the way it is."

"So do I," Nancy said, leaning against Ned's chest.

At just that moment, George walked into the kitchen. "Whoops," she said, sounding flustered. She backed out of the door. "I didn't mean to interrupt."

"You're not interrupting," Nancy said as Ned gave her one more quick hug. She followed George into the living room and told her what had happened.

George stared at her friend, dumbstruck. "Oh, Nan," she whispered, "that's awful! Somebody tried to blind you—right here, in the apartment!"

"It wasn't just me," Nancy said, with a shake of her head. "I mean, either one of you could have opened that cabinet door. The person who set that trap couldn't have guessed who would stumble on it first. No, whoever set this up wasn't particular. He was out to get any *one* of us."

"So, what do we do next?" Ned asked, crossing his arms.

Nancy looked at George. "Tomorrow," she declared, "George is going to visit a certain prominent plastic surgeon—about a nose job."

George's hand flew to her nose. "A nose job? No way! There's nothing wrong with my nose!"

Nancy laughed. "That's just the ploy we're going to use to get us into Emile Dandridge's office," she said, reaching for the phone. "I'll explain everything later. Oh, maybe I should ask Ms. Amberton to set up the appointment. She could get you in for sure."

As Nancy dialed, there was a knock on the door. Ned started toward it, but stopped when he saw a piece of folded paper being slipped under the closed door. Ned picked it up and read it, his eyes narrowing. He handed it to Nancy without a word.

Nancy put down the phone and opened the note. " 'If you're not concerned for your own safety, Nancy Drew,' " she read out loud, " 'perhaps you should worry about your two friends. How would you feel if one of them suddenly disappeared?' "

Chapter

Seven

CLUTCHING THE NOTE in her hand, Nancy leapt to the door and jerked it open. She looked up and down the corridor. The hallway was empty. There was no one in sight.

"Too late," Nancy said, coming back into the room. "He got away."

She sat down on the sofa and held the note under the lamp beside her, examining it closely. It was typewritten on a piece of plain cream-colored notepaper with a thin blue line printed down the left margin—nothing very significant there. But as Nancy turned it sideways, against the light, she noticed what seemed to be indentations in the paper.

"Look," she said, pulling out her magnifying glass, "I think this paper was under *another* piece of paper when somebody wrote on it.

Whatever was written on that top sheet left an impression here."

"Oh?" Ned asked, leaning over her shoulder. "What does it say?"

"I don't know," Nancy said. "I can't quite make it out." She glanced up. "We need some tissue paper."

"I bought a blouse today," George said. "The salesclerk wrapped it in tissue paper. What are you going to do with it?"

"An old detective trick," Nancy said. "Let's try a little scrap."

George got the tissue paper while Ned found a pencil. Then Nancy put the note down on the coffee table. Carefully, she laid the tissue paper on top of the impressions in the note and rubbed with the side of the pencil lead. As if by magic, the white shapes of letters emerged from a pencil-smudged background.

"Hey, that's neat," George exclaimed.

"But what does it *say?*" Ned asked.

"There're numbers," Nancy replied, peering closer. "Looks like five hundred, and then the letters *mg.* Then there are some letters I can't make out, and then *m-y-c-i-n.*"

George frowned. "Sounds like a chemical."

Suddenly Nancy looked up, smiling. "That's it! Five hundred milligrams of something-*mycin!* It's a prescription for some sort of antibiotic!"

"The doctor's office again!" Ned cried, snapping his fingers.

"Exactly," Nancy agreed. "Another lead. I think we're on the right track, don't you? The sooner we talk to that doctor, the better."

George touched her nose again. "As long as he doesn't do anything to my nose," she said defensively. She shot Nancy a pleading look.

"Don't worry, George. He won't get anywhere near your nose. Honest." Nancy glanced again at the threatening note. What would she do if anything happened to either one of her friends? The thought was too frightening.

"Look, this blackmailer is obviously determined to cause some damage—and he doesn't care *who* gets hurt."

"We're not worried, Nancy," Ned said playfully. "If anything happens, you'll protect us."

"Thanks a lot." Nancy rolled her eyes. But she knew Ned and George understood. "Now, maybe we should get to work." She reached for the phone and dialed Ms. Amberton's number.

"You nearly missed me," Ashley Amberton said, when Nancy reached her. "I was going to leave a little early."

"I'm sorry to call so late," Nancy apologized. "But I need to ask you to set up an appointment for me."

"Oh?"

"Yes, with a man named Emile Dandridge —Dr. Emile Dandridge."

There was a short silence. "Dr. Dandridge? The plastic surgeon?" Ms. Amberton replied. There was an odd note in her voice. "Why do you want to see him?"

Nancy told her about the conversation she and Ned had had with Lake Sinclair. She also mentioned that she was beginning to suspect someone in the doctor's office was blackmailing Lake.

"And when we got back to the apartment," Nancy went on, "I opened a cabinet door and narrowly missed getting a splash of liquid nitrogen in my face."

"You're all right, aren't you?" Ms. Amberton asked quickly. "You're not hurt?"

"Oh, no," Nancy reassured her. "If it hadn't been for Ned, though, I might have been blinded or badly burned."

"Was there any damage to the stove?" Ms. Amberton asked. Hurriedly, she cleared her throat and added, "Or to the rest of the kitchen? Shall I get the locks changed?"

"No, everything's okay," Nancy said. "Although you might want to change the locks. There's more, too." When she finished telling her about the note, and the impression of the prescription she had discovered, Ms. Amberton gave a loud exclamation of surprise.

"I must admit, Nancy Drew," she said with

grudging admiration, "that you are a *very* perceptive young woman. I didn't expect—I mean, it's quite amazing that you were able to trace down the connection to Dr. Dandridge with such slim clues. I'm quite impressed."

"How about that appointment? You could tell him that George wants to see him about getting her nose fixed."

"I'll do it immediately," Ms. Amberton promised. "And, Nancy, congratulations."

"For what?" Nancy asked, surprised.

"Why, on your narrow escape, of course," Ms. Amberton said.

Nancy hung up, a puzzled frown on her face.

"What's wrong?" George asked. "Isn't she going to make the appointment?"

Nancy nodded, still frowning.

"Then what is it?" Ned demanded.

Nancy shook her head. "Nothing, I suppose." There was something, some tiny thing that seemed out of place. But Nancy couldn't think of what it was.

"Well, then, wouldn't you say it's time for dinner?" he asked. He turned to George. "And I think it's George's turn to pick the place to eat."

Dr. Dandridge's office was in a low, modern building that was secluded behind a high brick wall in the most fashionable part of town. The receptionist was sitting beside a bank of tall palms and exotic flowers at one end of a teak-paneled room, furnished with elegant chairs and sofas and luxurious Persian rugs. Several people were already waiting to see the doctor when Nancy and George arrived for George's ten-thirty appointment.

George gave her name to the receptionist, and she nodded immediately. "Yes, of course," she said. "Ms. Amberton called late yesterday afternoon. If you'll just have a seat, I'll let the doctor know you're here."

She came back less than a minute later. "Dr. Dandridge will see you now," she said. The other patients all glared at Nancy and George as the receptionist led them down a carpeted hallway.

"Oh, by the way," she said, "please tell Ms. Amberton that the staff enjoyed the candy she brought over last week. It was very kind of her to think of us—and so unexpected, too."

Nancy shot George a questioning look as they entered the doctor's office. It was even more luxurious than the waiting room. The two girls sat down in plush, upholstered chairs.

As soon as the nurse left, Nancy turned to George. "I never would have imagined that Ms. Amberton was the kind of person who would bring candy to a doctor's staff—or flowers to a sick employee."

"Well, maybe she's not the coldhearted career woman she seems to be," George suggested. She got up and wandered over to look at the framed diplomas that hung on one wall. There were lots of them.

"How does anybody ever have time enough to study for all those final exams?" she asked, amazed. "This guy must *really* be smart!"

Nancy came to stand behind George. "And fast, too," she said, looking at the certificates. "According to these diplomas, he completed his residency six months after he got his medical degree. Usually it takes years."

"Good afternoon," a short, dapper-looking man said, coming through the door into the office. He was wearing a conservative navy blue suit instead of the usual white doctor's coat. Nancy thought he looked more like one of her father's lawyer friends than a doctor.

"I understand you wanted to see me about the possibility of undergoing a rhinoplasty," he said, adjusting his gold-rimmed glasses. "Which one of you is the patient?"

"A rhino—rhinoplasty?" George repeated in dismay. "Oh, it's nothing like *that*. I just want a nose job, that's all." She felt her nose. "You see, it's always been a little too long. And there's a hump in the middle where I got hit by a softball when I was ten."

Dr. Dandridge laughed. "My dear young woman," he said, "a rhinoplasty *is* a 'nose job,' as you put it." He sat down behind his desk.

"Oh." George walked back to the desk and sat down, too, flushing with embarrassment.

Nancy joined her. "Actually, Dr. Dandridge," she said, "I've been having trouble with my nose, too, lately."

Solicitously, the doctor leaned forward. "What kind of trouble?"

"I keep smelling something," Nancy replied. "Something terribly wrong."

"Well, we can examine you, too, young lady. Sometimes the sinus passages become blocked, and—"

"I'm not sure an examination would do any good, Doctor," Nancy explained, watching him closely. "Because what I keep smelling is blackmail."

"B-b-blackmail?" he stuttered, staring at Nancy.

"That's right," Nancy said. "You see, I'm a private detective. I've been hired by Cherbourg Industries to investigate a blackmailing ring. I have reason—very good reason—to believe that somebody in your office is the blackmailer."

"In my office?" Dr. Dandridge gulped. His face was white now. "What makes you think that?"

"One of the blackmail victims is a young

woman named Lake Sinclair. She's been paying the bills for the plastic surgery you've been
doing on a young girl. Lake claims that no one
knows about her involvement with your patient except the staff in your office—and you,
of course."

"Lake Sinclair is being blackmailed! But
that's not possible!" He picked up a small gold
keychain and began to turn it over nervously
in his fingers. In front of him, in a filigreed
silver holder, was a stack of cream-colored
notepaper with a thin blue line down the left
margin. "No. No, I simply don't believe it," he
said.

"Well, consider this then," Nancy told him,
standing. "Yesterday, there was an accident in
the apartment where we're staying. I was nearly burned with liquid nitrogen that spilled out
of a Thermos bottle in a cabinet over my head.
It was a frighteningly clever booby trap, and it
was set up by somebody with access to liquid
nitrogen."

"Yes, but any chemist could have provided
—" Dr. Dandridge began. His voice was thin
and panicky.

"Wait," Nancy cautioned. "There's more. A
few minutes after that I received a threatening
note. It was typed on cream-colored paper—
paper identical to that pad right in front of
you." She picked up a piece of the paper,
folded it carefully, and put it in her skirt

pocket. "I submit, Dr. Dandridge, that there is very good reason to believe that you or one of your staff is deeply involved with blackmail."

"Well, it isn't me!" the doctor exclaimed. The keys still in his hand, he stood up. "I have what you detectives call an airtight alibi. For the last two days, I've been in New York. I just got back this morning."

Nancy frowned. All the clues pointed to Dandridge. If it wasn't him, then it had to be one of his staff.

The doctor bent over and picked up an expensive-looking leather briefcase. He put it down flat on his desk. "Anyway," he said wearily, "there's another reason I can't be your blackmailer." He inserted one of the keys into the briefcase lock and began to open the lid.

Nancy tensed, and behind her George gasped out loud. What did he have in the briefcase? A gun? Slowly, the briefcase was opened. . . .

Chapter

Eight

MONEY!" GEORGE EXCLAIMED.

"There's fifty thousand dollars here," Dr. Dandridge said grimly. "It's the third installment—and I don't know how many more there'll be."

Nancy whistled softly. "Fifty thousand dollars!" Annette LeBeau, Lake Sinclair, Emile Dandridge—each of them paying tens of thousands of dollars. There was no question about it. Nancy had stumbled onto a big-time criminal operation that was netting somebody lots of money.

"See all this fine furniture?" Dr. Dandridge said, waving his arm. "Well, none of it belongs to me anymore. I've had to mortgage it. My office equipment, too. If it doesn't stop pretty soon, I'm going to be totally ruined."

Nancy turned around and glanced at the diplomas on the wall. "The blackmailer found out about your phony medical degrees, didn't he?"

Emile Dandridge stared at her. "How did you know?" he whispered.

Nancy shrugged and pointed to a diploma. "It wasn't hard to figure out," she said. "Nobody finishes a residency in six months."

Dr. Dandridge seemed to shrivel, Nancy thought, like a balloon after the air had been let out of it. "So *that's* how the blackmailer discovered it," he said wearily. "Why didn't I ever notice?" He went to the wall and took the diploma down, shaking his head. "I just never paid any attention to the dates."

"You don't even have a medical degree, do you?" Nancy asked.

"That's not true. I *did* graduate from medical school—in Mexico. My grades weren't good enough to get me into a Canadian school."

Nancy looked at him. "And you figured that a Mexican degree would turn off your wealthy clients. So, instead, you had someone forge a diploma from a prestigious American medical school."

Dr. Dandridge sank into the leather chair behind his desk. "The blackmailer must have seen the diplomas, just the way you did, and then checked it out. I'm sure there's no other

65

way it could have been discovered. I was very careful."

"That means that the blackmailer has been in this office," Nancy said. "I'll need to question your staff members. But first" —she looked at the briefcase filled with wrapped packets of bills—"you've been told to leave this money at Nelson's Column, right?"

Dr. Dandridge stared at her. "Exactly. I put the money into a red plastic bag and dump it in a trash can. How did you know?"

"It's the blackmailer's method," Nancy said. She glanced at the money again. "Is the drop scheduled for today?"

The doctor nodded. "At five o'clock," he said.

"George, this is it!" Nancy told her friend excitedly. "It's just what we've been waiting for—a real break!"

"What do you want me to do?" Dr. Dandridge asked.

"Go ahead with the drop, exactly as you've been instructed. But our blackmailer's going to have some company. When he picks up the money, we'll be there to pick *him* up."

"If the blackmailer is one of Dr. Dandridge's staff, it won't be a 'him,'" George reminded her.

"Oh, that's right," Nancy said. "The blackmailer could be a woman." She turned to the doctor. "I'd like to talk to your staff now. One at a time, please."

Nancy and George didn't learn a thing from the doctor's staff—a receptionist and two nurses. It was hard to picture *any* of them as the blackmailer, Nancy decided. The receptionist was barely out of her teens. One of the nurses was a grandmother in her sixties, and the other had worked in the office for only a few days. They hardly seemed like killers, either. They were all genuinely surprised by Nancy's questions. And George's careful check of the office typewriters revealed nothing.

"What about the person your new nurse replaced?" Nancy asked the doctor when she was finished.

"I've just expanded the staff," he explained. "I've had to take on more patients in order to meet the blackmailer's demands, so I had to hire another nurse."

Nancy frowned in frustration as she and George left the office. "I just don't understand it," she said. "All of the clues—the liquid nitrogen, the notepaper, the blackmailing of Lake Sinclair—led to Dandridge's office. I'm afraid we've reached a dead end."

"Not quite," George said, her voice full of anticipation. "There's still the drop this afternoon." She was obviously looking forward to the action.

"Right," Nancy said. "We'd better tell Ned. And I've got to call Ashley Amberton to let her know about this new development."

Ms. Amberton sounded very impressed with Nancy's detective work. "You mean, you actually *spotted* the discrepancies in his diplomas yourself?" she asked in disbelief.

"That's right," Nancy said. "He admitted it, of course. But now we know that the blackmailer must have had access to Dr. Dandridge's office. Otherwise, he couldn't have known about the fake diploma."

"You are an incredibly astute young woman, Nancy," Ms. Amberton said. "I'll report your progress to Mr. Cherbourg when I see him this afternoon."

"Well, maybe I'll have an even better report this evening," Nancy said. "By then, we might even know who our blackmailer is!"

At five o'clock the rush-hour traffic was heavy and the plaza around Nelson's Column was crowded with tourists and people on their way home from work. It was beginning to drizzle, and lights were coming on in the late afternoon.

"Let's wait across the street, behind those

brick pillars," Nancy told George and Ned. She pointed to a large building on the other side of the street. "That way, we can watch what's going on in the plaza without being seen."

"There's Dr. Dandridge," George said excitedly as soon as they crossed the street.

Carrying a red plastic bag, the collar of his tan raincoat pulled up, the doctor was walking quickly across the plaza. He ducked around a knot of people standing in front of the column.

"Look!" Ned exclaimed. "He's making the drop!" Glancing quickly around the square, the doctor dropped the bag into the open trash can and hurried away.

"Okay," Nancy said. "Everybody watch closely! Our blackmailer's bound to be here soon. He wouldn't risk leaving that money in the trash can for very long."

While they were watching, a large green bus pulled up just across the street, blocking their view.

"Come on!" Nancy exclaimed. "We're going to have to get back across the street so we can see."

Together, they started to cross the crowded street, slick now from the rain. They wove through the traffic single file.

At the end of the line, George looked over

her shoulder. "Nancy! Ned!" she screamed. "Look out!"

Nancy, who was at the bus, turned and looked. Behind her, Ned gave a shout. A bright yellow Mercedes had just rounded the corner, its headlights glaring in the gathering dusk. It was headed straight for them!

Chapter

Nine

SUCKING IN HER breath, Nancy grabbed Ned and pulled him flat against the bus with herself. She felt a *swoosh* as the Mercedes brushed past them frighteningly close. A moment later it was gone, its taillights flickering around the corner.

George, who had moved in the opposite direction, asked, "Are you guys all right?"

"I'll live," Ned croaked. "Nancy, you okay?"

"Aside from being slightly squashed," Nancy said, brushing a damp curl away from her face, "I'm fine. But that was too close!"

"Yeah!" George cried angrily. "What did that idiot woman think she was doing, anyway? Driving like that in rush-hour traffic! She could have killed us!"

"That," Ned growled as they stepped onto the curb, "is exactly what she was trying to do."

Nancy nodded. "I can see you're thinking the same thing I am."

George brightened. "The yellow Mercedes! Lake Sinclair! She's no victim—she's our blackmailer. She came to get the money and decided to get us as well."

"Could be," Nancy agreed. "From the glimpse I got of the driver, it looked as if she had long auburn hair." Suddenly her head snapped up. "The money!" Nancy exclaimed and darted toward the trash can.

But it was too late. While Nancy, Ned, and George had been escaping from the yellow Mercedes, the money had vanished. The red plastic bag was nowhere in sight!

"Oh, no!" Nancy exclaimed, dejected. She dropped down on a bench beside the trash can, disappointment rushing through her. "This was our big chance to catch the black-mailer, and we blew it."

"I don't know about that," Ned remarked, shoving his hands into his pockets. "It looks to me as if the whole thing was pretty carefully planned, and it went off just like clockwork. I have to admit," he added with admiration, "that Lake Sinclair is a lot smarter than I thought she was."

"Yeah," Nancy said, nodding. "That brush

with the car was timed exactly, to keep us busy while the money was picked up. But we're forgetting one important thing."

George frowned. "What's that?"

"If the blackmailer was driving the car that nearly ran us down, who picked up the money?"

"You mean," George said, pushing a wet brown curl out of her face, "that Lake Sinclair *isn't* our blackmailer?"

"I didn't say that," Nancy said cautiously. "Maybe we're up against a team." She stood up. "Come on, you guys, we've got work to do."

"Where to?" Ned asked, falling in step beside her as George hurried to catch up to them.

"To Lake Sinclair's place," Nancy said determinedly. She quickened her pace. "She may not be our blackmailer, but that yellow Mercedes is the hottest lead we've got."

Through the wrought-iron gate, Nancy could see the yellow Mercedes parked in the shadowy brick courtyard beside Lake Sinclair's.

"How do we get in?" George asked. She craned her neck to see through the gate. The courtyard was surrounded by a six-foot brick wall.

"Easy," Nancy said, taking her lock-pick kit from her shoulder bag. "This is a pretty simple lock." She looked in both directions. The now-dark street was empty, the reflections of the streetlights shimmering silver in the puddles from the earlier rain. A moment later she pushed the gate open. "Come on."

In seconds, the three of them were inside the courtyard. Ned felt the hood of the car, then got down on his hands and knees and reached up inside the front.

"There's no way this car could have been driven in the last few hours," he reported, shaking his head. "The radiator's cold."

"I don't understand it," George said with a frown. She went around to the driver's side and peered in, cupping her hands around her face. "This *has* to be the car!" She reached down for the door handle.

"Don't touch that handle!" Nancy exclaimed—but not in time. The alarm on the car had begun to emit short, sharp blasts. George gasped and leaped back.

"The door handle was wired with an alarm," Nancy whispered urgently. "Come on! Let's get out of here before somebody finds us!"

But at that moment a door opened in the house and light spilled out. A shadowy figure stood outlined against the light.

"Don't move," Lake Sinclair cried viciously, "or I'll blow your heads off!" A gun glinted in her hand. "Line up against the car and put your hands on the top."

Cautiously, Nancy turned. "It's me, Lake," she said. "Nancy Drew."

"I don't care if you're the queen herself," Lake said, gesturing with the gun. "Line up! This is the second time today that somebody's tried to steal my car—and this time I've got you!"

"What do you mean, *you've* got *us?*" George exclaimed indignantly, putting both hands against the car. *"We've* got *you* is more like it. You nearly killed us a little while ago!"

"That's ridiculous," Lake snapped, coming a little closer. "I haven't been out of this house all day."

"She's not lying," Ned reminded George. "The car's cold, remember. It couldn't have been *this* Mercedes that nearly ran us down."

"Ran you down?" Lake asked, lowering her gun.

Nancy told her what had happened in front of the plaza after they turned around to face Lake. "We came over here," she added, "to check out your car. After all, the driver *did* have auburn hair—just like yours."

"The blackmailer tried to *kill* you?" Lake repeated.

Nancy shrugged. "Somebody did. And not for the first time, either." She looked at Lake.

"Did you say this was the *second* time today that somebody tried to steal your car?"

"That's right." Lake slipped the gun into her pocket. "I heard the alarm go off around three this afternoon. By the time I got out here, the thief was gone." She nodded toward the gate. "First thing in the morning, I'm having a better lock put on that gate."

"It certainly was a surprise," George said with relief, "when your car alarm went off."

Lake looked at George. "You're the one who wants to run in Olympic Stadium?" she asked.

George nodded vigorously. "I sure do."

"Listen," Lake said, with an embarrassed shake of her head, "I'm sorry about what happened just now. I'll see if I can arrange a pass."

"That'd be terrific!" George replied with a wide grin.

Lake turned toward the door. "Well, good night. And good luck! I hope you find this guy before I have to make another payment—I don't have much left to sell!"

Back at the apartment, Nancy was just unlocking the door as the telephone began to ring. It was Ashley Amberton.

"I just thought I'd check," she said. "What happened when you went to Nelson's Column this afternoon?"

Nancy sketched out the events of the afternoon and evening. "Now that we know it wasn't Lake's Mercedes that nearly ran us down," she said, finishing her story, "we'll try to find out just who the car really belonged to. It shouldn't be hard. There can't be that many yellow Mercedes in Montreal."

"How do you even know the car came from Montreal?" Ms. Amberton asked quickly. "Maybe you shouldn't waste valuable time trying to trace it."

"All our other leads have dried up," Nancy pointed out. "The car is the only thing we have to go on right now."

"Still," Ms. Amberton persisted, "it'll be like looking for a needle in a haystack."

"Don't worry—we'll find it," Nancy promised. "There are three of us to work on it."

Ms. Amberton sighed. "Well, if you think you must," she said. "But be careful. Remember that last warning. You wouldn't want anything to happen to your friends, would you?"

Finding the yellow Mercedes wasn't as easy as Nancy had thought it would be. Reasoning that the most obvious way to get a specific type of car would be to rent one, they started calling rental agencies the next day. It was one dead end after another. Not a single agency had a yellow Mercedes to rent. Even worse, nobody had any idea where one could be found.

It was already the middle of the afternoon, and they had called all the agencies in the phone book. George plopped down on the sofa and sighed dejectedly. "This is nothing but a wild-goose chase," she said.

Nancy thumbed through the Yellow Pages, thinking. "Wait," she said. "There's something we haven't thought of."

"What's that?" Ned asked, coming from the kitchen with three glasses of lemonade.

"What else? A Mercedes dealer!" Nancy exclaimed. "Maybe he'd know."

George shrugged. "Of course. And there seems to be only one dealer for this whole area," she said, handing the phone to Nancy.

"A yellow Mercedes?" the manager of the Mercedes dealership said when Nancy reached him. "Actually, it just so happens that I do have one on the lot. It's probably the only one for sale in Montreal." He laughed. "Yellow must be a very popular color this year."

"Really?" Nancy asked, suddenly even more interested. "What makes you say that?"

"Well, yesterday a man wanted to test-drive a Mercedes—but it had to be yellow. He brought it right back after the drive, and he said he didn't want it. It's still here and still as beautiful as ever."

"Hmmm," Nancy said. "Who was this man? I wonder if I know him."

"You might," the dealer replied. "He's a very influential man in Montreal."

"Oh?" Nancy sat tensed on the edge of the sofa. "What's his name?"

"I really shouldn't say," said the dealer. "But, oh, well, he was Pierre Cherbourg."

Chapter

Ten

Pierre Cherbourg!" Nancy exclaimed.

"Well, not Mr. Cherbourg himself, of course," the dealer added hurriedly. "I didn't deal with him directly. Just his chauffeur —Jacques Olivier—late yesterday afternoon. Now, when can I arrange a test-drive for you?" the dealer asked smoothly. "Would today be convenient?"

"No, not today," Nancy replied. "I have some other pressing business to attend to. I'll call later to make the appointment." She hung up.

"Mr. Cherbourg?" Ned and George asked in unison.

Nancy shook her head and reached for the lemonade Ned had brought. "It was the chauffeur," she said. "The dealer lent the car to Jacques Olivier."

"But wait, the driver had long auburn hair," Ned reminded them.

"It could have been a wig," Nancy replied with a shrug.

"Of course!" Ned exclaimed. "The chauffeur tried to steal Lake's car—and when he got scared off by the alarm, he borrowed one. And then he dressed up like Lake to fool us into thinking it was her behind the wheel!"

George shook her head. "This whole thing is too confusing," she said, frowning. "It's giving me a headache."

"Want to know the best cure for a headache?" Nancy asked, getting up. "Action!"

George's frown turned suspicious. "What kind of action?"

"Come on, gang. We're going to question a certain chauffeur!"

Jacques Olivier, Nancy learned from the personnel department at Cherbourg Industries, lived in a small white cottage behind the Cherbourg mansion. It was late afternoon by the time they got there. Nancy, with Ned and George right behind her, walked up the brick path that led to the doorstep of the cottage. To her left, Nancy could see the large garage. Inside was the Cherbourg limousine.

"I don't hear anything," George whispered after Nancy had knocked twice.

She knocked harder. "The car's here," she said. "I think he's hiding out."

Finally, after Nancy had knocked a fourth time, the door opened a tiny crack.

"Who is it?" Jacques asked. His voice was fearful.

"It's Nancy Drew," Nancy told him. "I need to talk to you."

The door slammed shut. "Go away," Jacques called, his voice muffled through the door. "I'm sick. I don't want to see anybody."

"But it's important," Nancy insisted. She hesitated. "If I can't talk to you, I suppose I'll have to go see Ms. Amberton—or maybe even Mr. Cherbourg."

"Nancy!" George hissed. "That's black-mail!"

"You bet," Nancy agreed grimly. "Fight fire with fire, I always say."

The door opened again, a little wider this time. "You wouldn't do that, would you?" Jacques whispered.

"I will if I don't get some answers," Nancy replied in a firm voice. He backed up and let them in.

All the curtains and shades had been drawn. Jacques was obviously hiding out. What was he afraid of?

The chauffeur closed the door behind them.

"What do you want to know?" he asked nervously.

"We want to know why you borrowed the yellow Mercedes from the Mercedes dealer," Nancy said.

Jacques's face paled. "But I didn't—"

"There's no use denying it," Nancy told him. "We've already talked to the dealer. He'll swear that you borrowed it." She looked around. "Where's the wig you wore when you nearly ran us down?"

Jacques sagged weakly into a chair. "I threw it away," he said in a broken voice. "Into the trash can."

"Speaking of trash cans," George said, "who took the money out of the trash can at Nelson's Column yesterday afternoon?"

"Money?" Jacques shook his head frantically, his eyes wide with fear. "I didn't take any money."

"Well, then," Nancy responded, "tell us what you *do* know."

"Somebody called me on the telephone yesterday at around noon," the chauffeur said. "I couldn't recognize the voice. I couldn't even tell whether it was a man or a woman. I was instructed to—" He swallowed hard. "I was instructed to—to borrow the yellow Mercedes belonging to Mademoiselle Sinclair."

"You mean, *steal* it, don't you?"

Jacques shifted uneasily. "I didn't want to

do it, mademoiselle," he said. "But the person said that if I followed his instructions, I would be free. There would be no more blackmail payments—ever!"

"So when you couldn't steal Lake Sinclair's car, you went to the Mercedes dealer," Nancy supplied. "And then you came after us."

"I was told you'd be in the plaza at five. I was told not to let you walk away." He thought for a moment, and then repeated miserably, "I didn't want to do it. Even though I wanted to be free of the blackmail, I couldn't bring myself to kill you."

"You mean you missed us on purpose?" Ned asked.

"At the last moment I swerved."

"It's a good thing you did, too," Nancy said. "If you'd hit us, it would have been a cinch for the police to track you down in that car. The blackmailer knew what he was doing. You were a sitting duck."

Jacques nodded. "I am sorry," he whispered again.

In the taxi on their way back to the apartment, Nancy stared out the window, thinking. "You know," she said after they had climbed out and Ned paid the driver, "maybe we were tricked."

"How?" Ned asked, pocketing the change.

"Maybe last night's drop was a phony—set

up to lure us to the plaza. Maybe *we* were the sitting ducks, and the blackmail money was just a decoy."

"You might have something there," George said. They got into the elevator and pushed the button for the sixth floor.

"If that's true," Ned remarked, "then Dandridge would have to be in on it."

"Maybe Dandridge *is* in on it," Nancy said. "Maybe he set the whole thing up. When we confronted him in his office, he could have shown us that money just to throw us off—to convince us that he was a victim, too."

"Sure!" George exclaimed. "Then he could have called Jacques Olivier and arranged to have him run us down!"

"That makes sense," Ned said slowly. "In fact, Dandridge is the only one who knew that we were going to be there at five o'clock." He pulled out his key to the apartment and opened the door.

Nancy frowned. "It *does* make sense, but—" Something was nagging at the back of her mind. What *was* it?

"Listen, you guys," George said, dropping wearily onto a chair, "I'm ready to stop exercising my brain for a few hours and exercise my stomach. What do you say to some dinner?"

"Yeah, I'm starving." Ned grinned. "Do you have somewhere in mind?" he asked.

"Well, it just so happens," George said airily, "that Pierre works in a *great* restaurant."

"But we've already had so much French food," Nancy objected.

"Actually, it's a Greek restaurant. Over on Prince Arthur Street."

"What's a guy named Pierre doing working in a Greek restaurant?" Ned asked with a laugh.

"Beats me." George shrugged. "Anyway, we had lunch there the other day and the food is terrific!" She kissed the tips of her fingers. "What do you say?"

Nancy giggled and turned to Ned. "How do you say yes in Greek?" she asked.

"You got me," Ned confessed.

"Well, then, I guess I'll just have to say *oui,*" Nancy replied, and they all laughed.

The food *was* terrific, Nancy agreed after she had finished her dolmas, Greek salad, and slice of rich, sweet baklava for dessert. Afterward, there was live bouzouki music. Then Pierre, who Nancy decided was really cute, joined them for dancing. Yawning, Nancy and Ned said their good nights early, leaving George in the arms of her Frenchman. They held hands as they walked back to the apartment in the soft spring night, talking quietly and admiring the lighted shop windows.

"It really *was* a terrific evening," Nancy said when they got back to the apartment.

"Yeah," Ned agreed softly. "And you know, I'm not tired anymore. Let's see if we can find some good music to dance to."

Nancy smiled. "Good idea," she said. Ned fiddled with the tuning knob for a moment. The station he got was playing one of their favorite love songs. Nancy nodded to Ned, and when he stood back up, she went into his arms. The two of them danced slowly around the living room.

"You're so wonderful," Ned whispered into Nancy's hair. His arms tightened around her.

Nancy felt herself growing breathless as she leaned against Ned's chest. "So are you, Nickerson."

Gently, Ned leaned down and touched his lips to hers. "Oh, Nancy," he whispered, "I—"

Just then there was a knock on the door. Nancy pulled away and started for it. "Somebody's got an absolutely *rotten* sense of timing."

Ned shook his head. "It's pretty late for anybody to stop by," he told her, putting his hand on Nancy's arm. "Let me handle this."

"But—" she started to protest.

"Listen, after all the things that have happened in the past few days," Ned whispered firmly, "I'm not taking *any* chances." He stepped in front of Nancy. "Who is it?" he called loudly.

There was no answer.

"Who is it?" Ned called again, more sharply.

"The porter," came the muffled reply.

"Stand back," Ned ordered Nancy. "This could be dangerous." Then slowly, cautiously, making sure that the chain was hooked, he began to open the door.

Chapter

Eleven

"HERE YOU ARE, sir," the man said. "This arrived for you just now."

"Don't tell me," Nancy groaned. "It's another threatening letter."

"I don't think so," Ned said, looking at the white envelope he had been handed. "This one has a return address on it. It's from Lake Sinclair—to all three of us."

"Well, then, open it," Nancy commanded.

Ned opened the envelope and took out two red tickets and a green one. "Hey, they're passes!" he exclaimed. "To get into Olympic Stadium."

Nancy took the passes from him. "The green one is for George," she said, reading the fine print. "It lets her onto the track. And the red ones get us into the press box. But they're only good from eleven to twelve tomorrow. That's weird."

"And here's a note," Ned said, reaching back into the envelope. "'Here are your passes,'" he read. "'Nancy and Ned can watch from the press box while George makes her debut appearance in Olympic Stadium.' It's signed 'Lake.'"

The door opened as George let herself into the apartment. She looked dreamy and starry eyed. "Hi," she said vaguely, hardly noticing them. She drifted toward the bedroom.

Nancy reached out and grabbed the sleeve of George's sweater. "Hey, George, we've got something for you," she said.

"That's nice," she said, stopping.

Nancy waved the pass in front of her friend's eyes. "Drew calling Fayne," she said. "Drew calling Fayne. Come in, please."

"Huh?" George's eyes refocused. "What'd you say?"

Ned laughed. "We said that Lake got us those passes. You'll get your chance to run in Olympic Stadium."

George squealed and grabbed the pass, jumping up and down with excitement. "I can't believe it!"

"And we'll be there to watch," Nancy said. "We've got passes to the press box."

"Speaking of tomorrow," Ned said, looking at Nancy, "what's on the agenda?"

Nancy sat down on the sofa and pulled her knees up under her chin. "Well, I've been thinking," she said. "About Dandridge, that is."

"What about him?" George asked.

"We definitely can't strike him off our list of suspects. There's every possibility that yesterday's drop was a dummy."

"So what do you want to do?" Ned asked, sitting down beside Nancy.

"We're going to question him again," Nancy said. "First thing in the morning. If he's been telling us the truth, his bank account should show some very large cash withdrawals—and no substantial deposits."

"While you're doing that," George broke in, "I hope you don't mind if I go out with Pierre. Tomorrow's his day off, and he wants to show me the view from Mont-Royal. I could go to the stadium from there and meet you after my run."

Nancy stared at her friend in mock anger. "You know, it's a good thing I don't have to depend on *you* to solve this case, Fayne."

"Well, you can't blame a girl for falling in love, can you?" George said dreamily.

"So you don't believe what I've told you?" Dr. Dandridge growled. He had agreed to meet Nancy and Ned in his office the next morning even though it was Saturday. "You

91

still insist that I've got something to do with this blackmail business?"

Nancy smiled pleasantly. "Right now there are just too many loose ends to permit me to draw *any* conclusions, Dr. Dandridge. However, there is a way you could help us tie some of them up."

The doctor frowned. "Just what did you have in mind, Ms. Drew?"

"Your bank account should be a complete record of your dealings with the blackmailer. We'd like to see it."

Dr. Dandridge looked shocked. "My bank account? You want my personal records?"

"Actually, it would be easier if you just called an officer at your bank," Nancy told him. "I could review the account there and save you the inconvenience of digging out your statements."

Dr. Dandridge sighed and reached for the phone. "If this is the only way to convince you," he said, "then it's worth it. Fortunately, my bank is open on Saturday mornings."

On the way to the bank, Nancy stopped to call Ms. Amberton at her home to bring her up to date on what they'd done the day before, and on their talk with the doctor. But she wasn't home.

"It was okay," Nancy told Ned. "I just left a message telling her that we found out who was driving the yellow Mercedes. That should interest her."

"You understand, of course, that this is extremely irregular," the bank manager said. He was dressed in a conservative black suit and vest, and his hair was thinning on top. "It is highly unusual to give out information on other people's accounts."

"But you had Dr. Dandridge's phone call," Nancy assured him smoothly. "And I've also brought you a signed request."

"Yes, of course," the manager said with a sigh. He cleared his throat. "Well, then, here is a summary of the activity in the account." He handed a computer printout to Nancy. "I must say, I have been puzzled by the recent large cash withdrawals from this account."

Nancy scanned the printout. She spotted the withdrawals right away. They exactly corresponded to what Dr. Dandridge had told them.

"This is the only account the doctor has with this bank?" she asked, just to be sure.

"The only one," the manager said. "With the exception of his loan account, of course." He shifted uneasily. "A rather *large* loan, as a matter of fact."

"Well, then, I think we've found what we came for," she told the manager and stood up.

* * *

"So, we can scratch Dandridge as a suspect," Ned remarked as they threaded their way through the crowd of afternoon shoppers on Saint-Antoine Street.

"I suppose so," Nancy said, stopping to eye a fashionable flowered sundress in a shop window. "His bank account confirms what he's already told us. Too bad—he was such a promising suspect. I mean, just look at the clues!"

"Yeah," Ned said, linking his arm in hers as they started to walk again. "First the liquid nitrogen, then the impression of the prescription written on notepaper from *his* desk."

"And don't forget that he knew we'd be in the plaza at five," Nancy added. "Everything definitely points to Dandridge. It's almost as if somebody wanted us to suspect him. But here we are, up against a stone wall." She shook her head gloomily. "And we thought this was going to be such an easy case."

A clock in a nearby church struck the half hour.

"Hey, it's ten-thirty," Ned said. "We'd better hurry if we want to see George run in the stadium." He tugged at Nancy's arm. "I want to stop by the apartment and get my camera. We have to get pictures of this!"

Nancy and Ned got out of the taxi at the edge of Olympic Park. Before them loomed a huge oval stadium. It was made of concrete and steel and supported by V-shaped concrete ribs.

"It's huge!" Nancy exclaimed, staring up at the gigantic building. Standing beside one of the massive supporting ribs, she felt tiny.

"Over here," Ned said, pointing to a sign that said Press Entrance. He slid his camera case higher on his shoulder. "The press box must be this way."

They presented their passes to the guard at the gate, who looked at them curiously.

"Where'd you get these passes?" he demanded.

"From Lake Sinclair," Nancy told him.

"Oh, that's fine, then," he said, his face relaxing. "We don't usually let people into the building except on guided tours." He shrugged. "Someone else with a pass came through here a few minutes ago. She a friend of yours?"

"That must be George," Ned said. "Come on, Nancy! I want to see the inside of this thing."

The stadium seemed even larger inside than it had from the outside—maybe because it was absolutely empty. The press box was a long glass booth along one side of the open-roofed structure. From there they had a bird's-eye view of the track, far below. The far side of the track was over a hundred yards away.

Nancy sat down at the table along the window, holding an imaginary microphone in her hand.

"Ladies and gentlemen," she said, "we're here in world-famous Olympic Stadium to watch the running debut of Ms. Georgia Fayne, international champion jogger. Beneath us is the track, where Ms. Fayne will perform. Above us we can see the sky. All around us are empty seats—rows and rows of empty seats."

Ned laughed. "Almost sixty thousand empty seats," he said. He opened his camera bag and carefully removed a long lens, fitting it onto his camera. "This is a great place to try out my new telephoto lens," he said enthusiastically.

"Oh, look, Ned!" Nancy exclaimed, pushing up the sleeves of her red blouse. "There's George! Doesn't she look tiny down there?"

George came into view far below, moving swiftly from left to right around the track. She was wearing an Olympic running shirt and red, white, and blue shorts. Nancy waved as her friend passed in front of the press box, but George didn't look up.

As Nancy turned back to Ned, who was still busy with his camera, she noticed a second person coming down the ramp at the far end of the stadium. Apparently, George was going to have company on the track because the person was dressed in a white jogging jacket with the hood pulled up.

Ned stopped fiddling with his lens and raised the camera to his eye. "Hey, neat," he said, looking around the track. "Just like a telescope."

"What do you see?" Nancy wanted to know.

"Well, George certainly has great legs," Ned replied, a hint of teasing laughter in his voice.

Nancy grinned and gave him a playful shove. "Hey, what about *my* legs?" she asked, pouting.

Ned turned, pointing his camera at Nancy's legs. He whistled. "Wow!" he said admiringly. *"Some* legs."

"What I really want to know about is that other runner," Nancy said, directing his attention back to the track.

Ned swiveled his camera. "I can't tell about her legs. Or maybe his," he reported with a grin. The other runner was almost opposite them then, on the far side of the track. George was catching up fast. "That's strange," Ned remarked.

"What? What's strange?" Nancy asked, watching George, who was now almost on the heels of the other runner.

Ned shrugged. "That runner's wearing white gloves and carrying a can of hair spray or something."

"Gloves? Hair spray?" Nancy exclaimed,

alarmed. "Let me see!" She jerked the camera away from Ned and looked through the view-finder.

Just as Nancy got the camera focused, George flashed into view on the right side of the frame, right behind the runner.

"Ned!" Nancy exclaimed. "That's no can of hairspray! It's—"

Nancy and Ned watched helplessly as the gloved runner whirled around, grabbed George's arm with one hand, and pushed the can toward George's face.

Stumbling, George raised her hands and rubbed her eyes. Then she took two steps and collapsed.

Chapter

Twelve

IT LOOKS LIKE tear gas or something!" Nancy yelled. On the track, George was gasping frantically and tearing at her eyes.

Ned jumped up, knocking his chair over, and bolted for the door. In an instant he was clattering down the long, steep stairway toward the field far below. Nancy followed as fast as she could. Ned was a super-fast runner, though, and he was rapidly outdistancing her. Already he had reached the lowest tier of seats.

Down on the track, George was struggling to sit up. The attacker bent over her for a moment, and then George fell back, not moving.

The runner bent over and hoisted the now-limp George into a fireman's carry, straightening up with difficulty. Once the attacker was standing upright, George's weight seemed to be an easier burden. Carrying George, the white-jacketed figure shuffled to a nearby tunnel and disappeared.

Ned finally reached the end of the aisle and vaulted over the rail and onto the track. At a dead run he raced across the field toward the exit where George and her attacker had vanished. But just as Ned reached the mouth of the tunnel, Nancy heard the echoing screech of car tires, and her heart sank. Running was no use anymore—George was gone.

George was gone! Suddenly the reality of it hit Nancy. George had been kidnapped! Where was she being taken? *Who* had taken her?

Her heart pounding painfully, Nancy jogged down the track to the spot where George had fallen. There was something on the track: the empty can and a syringe. Nancy shook her head. There was no use looking for fingerprints on the can or the syringe—the white gloves would have taken care of that. Like everything else in this case, the kidnapping had been carefully planned and beautifully executed. There was no doubt about it. They were dealing with a first-rate criminal mind, and so far it had defeated them at every turn. It was almost as if they were playing some sort of game.

But it was a deadly game now. There was a life at stake. George's life.

Ned ran back to Nancy, panting. From the look on his face, Nancy knew he hadn't seen a thing.

"It's no use," he gasped, out of breath. "Whoever it was—had everything planned perfectly. All I could see was a pair of taillights disappearing around the corner. I didn't even see the car. The garage was too dark."

"Well, we know one thing," Nancy said. "The kidnapper had to be a man. George is no featherweight."

"Not so fast," Ned cautioned. "A woman could have managed to carry her with that fireman's carry. All the weight is over your back and legs. You could carry me if you had to." He shook his head. "No, it still could be a woman, Nancy."

"Whoever it is, he—or she—is a pro," Nancy said, picking up the syringe carefully. "This was probably loaded with some kind of quick-acting sedative. Once George was blinded by the tear gas, she was knocked out with this."

"Now what?" Ned asked as they made their way back up to the press box to pick up Ned's camera. "Do we call the police and report a kidnapping?"

"Only if we have to," Nancy replied grimly.

"We know more about this case than the police could find out in a week. But there is one person we have to check out, and on the double."

"Oh?" Ned asked. "Who's that?"

Soberly Nancy looked at Ned. "Who knew we were going to be here this afternoon?"

Ned shook his head. "Nobody. Except Lake Sinclair, that is. She had to because she arranged the passes for us."

"Right. And remember the first time we met her? She was wearing a white jogging suit, just like the top the attacker had on. There was a weight room in her condo, too. If it was a woman who kidnapped George, it could have been Lake."

"Passes?" Lake gasped in surprise. She was standing in the middle of her kitchen, surrounded by trays and platters of food. "I didn't arrange any passes for you. I meant to, but I didn't have time. I've been too busy getting ready for my party tonight."

"If *you* didn't, then who did?" Ned asked.

"The blackmailer, of course," Nancy said wearily. "Remember the letter I got? Obviously, he's made good on his threat to hurt you or George."

"If you need proof that I wasn't involved," Lake added, picking up a tray of tiny sandwiches, "ask anyone here." She turned to a white-aproned caterer who was working behind her at the stove. "Tell these people where I've been all morning, Philippe."

"She's been right here in the kitchen, mademoiselle," Philippe answered in surprise. "Of course."

"Well, that's that," Nancy said. It was nearly two, and she and Ned had just gotten back to the apartment. "It's obvious that Lake really didn't have anything to do with George's disappearance." She looked around the apartment. It seemed so empty without George.

Nancy picked up the phone. "I'd better let Ms. Amberton know what's happened." She was still out, so Nancy left another message to tell her that George had disappeared.

Nancy put the phone down with a sigh. "I guess there's nothing to do now but wait." She stretched wearily out on the sofa, her hands behind her head. "The kidnapper's bound to get in touch with us, sooner or later."

"Well, while we're waiting," Ned said, "I vote for a sandwich. We never even ate lunch. How about it?"

"I think there are some cold cuts in the refrigerator," Nancy said. "And some soda."

They had just settled down to the salami

sandwiches Ned had made when there was a knock on the door.

"Delivery service," someone called.

"We're not expecting anything," Nancy said to Ned in a low voice.

Cautiously Ned went to the door and opened it as far as the chain would allow. "It *is* a delivery," he reported. "A plastic box."

"Where'd you get this?" Nancy asked, coming up behind Ned.

The boy shrugged. "Don't know," he replied. "It came to the office just a little while ago, with instructions to deliver immediately." He thrust a clipboard at Ned. "Sign here, please."

Nancy looked at the box Ned held in his hand. "That looks like a videocassette!" she exclaimed.

Ned opened the box. "It *is* a tape." He looked at the VCR sitting on top of the television set. "I'll put it in."

Nancy adjusted the television set as Ned put the tape on. They both sat down on the sofa with the remote control and Ned flicked it on.

For a moment the screen was filled with silvery snow. Then the image cleared and Nancy could see George. She was seated, tied to a chair. She was pale and obviously groggy, but her eyes were open and filled with terror. There was a smear of blood on her cheek.

"Oh, no," Nancy moaned. "Poor George!" She wanted to look away, but she couldn't. It was hypnotizing.

Ned stared at the screen, his fists clenched, trying to speak. No words would come out. On the tape, a thickly muffled voice said, "Well, Nancy Drew, did you enjoy the view from the press box?" Nancy couldn't tell whether it was a man or a woman, but there was no disguising the triumph in it.

The kidnapper chuckled. "Wasn't that an interesting show? Of course, now that I have your friend, I have to decide what to do with her. I have lots of choices, but I haven't made up my mind—yet. But if you'll go out to Sainte-Hélène's Island now, to the museum at the Old Fort, I'll get in touch with you. Wait there to hear from me." There was a moment of silence, and then the chuckle came again. The screen went black.

Shakily, Nancy got to her feet. "Oh, Ned," she whispered. "This is so awful. And I feel responsible."

Ned put his arm around her shoulders. "I feel pretty awful, too," he said in a low voice. "But you can't blame yourself."

For a few moments Nancy let Ned's comforting arms surround her. Then she pulled back. "Well, we can't think about that now," she said in a determined voice. "We've got to think about George and how to get her back. Come on. Let's go to the Old Fort."

The Old Fort wasn't a fort at all, Nancy and Ned discovered. Instead it was a protected grassy area on Saint-Hélène's Island that was used as an arsenal back in 1822. Also on the island were some of the pavilions left over from Expo '67. They'd been turned into shops and restaurants and cafés, along with swimming pools, gardens—even an aquarium.

But Nancy and Ned didn't care to shop or to see the sights. They hurried directly to the museum, a two-story building that housed displays tracing the history of New France and Canada through the early days. It was filled with weapons, brightly colored military uniforms, and a large model of what Montreal was like in 1760.

Nancy paced nervously back and forth in the lobby. "What's the kidnapper going to do with her?"

"I don't know," Ned said sympathetically and glanced at the phone at the information desk. "Do you suppose the kidnapper will call?"

"That's a possibility," Nancy said. "But with this guy, you can't tell. He might try anything! Or she," she added, remembering that the kidnapper could be a woman.

It was nearly five o'clock, and Nancy was

beginning to feel desperate. What would happen if the museum closed and the kidnapper hadn't contacted them yet? But just then the telephone on the desk rang. The woman who answered it looked around at the few people left in the lobby.

"Is there someone here named Nancy Drew?" she asked in a thick French accent.

Nancy jumped for the phone, with Ned right beside her. The kidnapper laughed, a grating sound that echoed in Nancy's ear. "Are you and your friend enjoying the museum?" the voice asked.

"What have you done with George?" Nancy demanded. "Where is she?"

"Ah, so the famous detective is stumped at last!" the voice exclaimed, obviously pleased. "Well, Nancy Drew, you'll just have to wait until I'm ready to tell you where she is—and I'm not ready yet." The voice dropped, and there was an edge to it that made Nancy's blood run cold. "But you can be sure of one thing, my dear detective."

"What's that?" Nancy whispered.

"George Fayne is going to die. And you and Ned are, too. The game is mine, my friend, and I get to make up the rules!"

Chapter
Thirteen

THERE WAS NOTHING for Nancy and Ned to do but go back to the apartment. They didn't dare go out to dinner in case the kidnapper called. Instead, they ordered a pizza and ate it without really tasting it. They watched television without really seeing it, and neither of them said a word.

The phone startled them both when it rang. Nancy jumped to answer it while Ned turned down the TV. But it wasn't the kidnapper—it was Annette LeBeau. Nancy sighed nervously. She didn't want to tie up the line.

"I've been out of town for a few days," Annette said, "and when I got back this evening I received the strangest phone call."

"A phone call?" Nancy asked.

"Yes. Someone—I'm not sure whether it

was a man or a woman—wanted me to call you with a message." Nancy heard a rustling of paper. "I wrote it down so I could give it to you exactly."

With growing excitement, Nancy reached for a pencil. The message had to be from the kidnapper. "Okay," she said eagerly. "Let's hear it."

"'Nancy and Ned are going to have a lovely day sightseeing tomorrow,'" Annette read. "'The view from Mont-Royal is the best in the city. The Chalet is the place to wait.'" She cleared her throat. "Do you mind if I ask you what this is all about?" she added curiously.

Nancy's jaw tightened. "Our blackmailer has added a new crime to his repertoire," she said grimly. "Kidnapping."

"Kidnapping!"

"Our friend George Fayne was kidnapped this morning from Olympic Stadium."

"Have you called the police?"

"No, not yet," Nancy replied. "But if we don't have any leads by tomorrow, we may have to."

"Well, if I can help in any way, just let me know," Annette said. "The resources of the station are at your disposal, if they would help."

Nancy thanked Annette and put down the telephone. Then she remembered to call Ms. Amberton to update her. After hanging up she said to Ned slowly, "You know, this whole thing feels like some sort of scavenger hunt. It's as if we've been following a trail of clues that somebody deliberately laid out for us. And *George* is the grand prize." She looked down at her notes. "Tomorrow, we're supposed to look for clues at the top of Mont-Royal."

Nancy and Ned spent most of the next day, Sunday, in the mountaintop park, in the center of the city. But it was as fruitless as the afternoon they spent on Sainte-Hélène's Island. No call, nothing.

The view *was* stunning, though. They could pick out the Cherbourg Building in the middle of the other skyscrapers in downtown Montreal. To their left was the oval of Olympic Stadium. The distance made it look tiny.

But Nancy and Ned spent the entire, endless day sitting on the terrace in the Chalet near the pay phone. They kept going over and over the details of the case.

"I feel so helpless," Nancy told Ned. It was five-thirty in the afternoon and getting cool. She pulled her yellow cardigan closer around her. "I feel like a puppet on a string, jumping whenever the kidnapper says jump. I'm sure this creep is our blackmailer, too," she added bitterly.

Ned shaded his eyes from the late-afternoon sun as he looked toward the river. He pointed to the wharves. "You know what," he said. "Those big warehouses along the river would make a great hiding place. I wonder if George is in one of those buildings along the docks."

Nancy leaned both elbows on the table, shrugging. "I've decided," she said, "that the kidnapper-blackmailer is sending us on these wild-goose chases just to keep us busy."

"Maybe we were getting too close," Ned suggested. "Maybe the blackmailer got nervous."

"Exactly where *are* we?" Nancy asked thoughtfully. "We've eliminated Emile Dandridge and Lake Sinclair as suspects, we've established that—"

The telephone on the wall rang, interrupting her.

"It's the kidnapper!" Nancy exclaimed, dashing for it. "I'm sure of it!"

But when she picked up the phone, she was greeted by Ashley Amberton's voice. "I just received a telephone message, instructing me to call you at this number," Ms. Amberton said. "We're supposed to be in my office in exactly thirty minutes," she said. "I'm at home now, but I'll meet you there in a half hour. You'll receive another message when we get to the office."

111

Nancy looked at her watch. "We're on our way," she said.

"Oh, and Nancy—there's more to the message. Something very odd."

"What is it?" Nancy asked.

"It says, 'Playing blindman's buff has been fun, but the game's getting boring. Isn't it time you cried *uncle?*'"

The Sunday afternoon traffic was heavier than Nancy had expected, and it was nearly six-thirty when Nancy and Ned finally got to Ashley Amberton's office.

"You just missed the call," she told them, greeting Nancy and shaking hands with Ned. Nancy noticed that her left hand was bandaged. She wondered what had happened.

"What did the kidnapper say?" Nancy asked eagerly.

"Here's the message," Ms. Amberton said, giving it to Nancy with a chilly smile. "I copied it down exactly."

"What does it say, Nan?" Ned asked.

"'Your friend is all packed up and ready to go at the Cherbourg Wharf,'" Nancy read out loud. "'If you don't find her by midnight, she's going to be taking a short ocean trip—*straight down.*'"

Ashley Amberton glanced at her watch. "I've taken the liberty," she said, "of arranging for the company helicopter to fly you over to the wharf. It's waiting for you on the roof right now. Traffic is heavy at this hour, and the helicopter will have you on the wharf in no time at all. Since you'll be flying in, you won't have to worry about the gates, which are locked, of course. It's a high-security area."

"What about the warehouse?" Nancy asked. "Is it locked, too?"

Ms. Amberton opened her desk drawer. "This should do the trick." She handed Nancy a ring of keys. One was marked Warehouse.

Nancy thrust the keys into the pocket of her flower-printed skirt. "Thanks," she said. She and Ned followed Ms. Amberton to the elevator.

Up on the roof the helicopter was ready to go. Its rotor blades turned lazily as the pilot warmed the engine. When he saw them coming, he gunned the engine and the rotors began to spin more quickly. The stiff wind almost blew Nancy over as she ran across the roof, Ned right behind her.

"One more thing," Ashley Amberton said as the pilot reached down to give Nancy a hand. "As soon as you find her, I want you to bring your friend here so that I know she's safe. I'll stay here and work."

"We will," Nancy promised. "Will you please call the police and have them meet us at

the warehouse? We'll need help searching."
The older woman nodded. "And thanks again
for everything you've done."

"You've got nothing to thank me for," Ms.
Amberton said with a smile. "Now hurry!
You've got to get over to the wharf fast, before
your friend is murdered!"

Chapter

Fourteen

THE HELICOPTER FLEW out over the choppy
surface of the Saint Lawrence River, carrying
Nancy and Ned to the Cherbourg Wharf.
Darkness was falling, and the lights of Montreal were flickering on like a web of sparkling
diamonds far below. It was like riding a magic
carpet, Nancy thought. It might have even
been fun if she hadn't kept thinking about the
kidnapper's ominous message. At midnight,
George would be killed! But at least, thanks
to Ms. Amberton, they weren't wasting
time just trying to get to the wharf. That left
more time to look for George. She checked
her watch. It was just after seven, In the
seat beside her, Ned was looking out the
window.

"That's the Cherbourg warehouse down there!" the pilot yelled into her ear over the deafening clatter of the copter's rotors.

Below, Nancy could just make out the dim outline of a very long, narrow building. It took up at least three acres of dock space. Beside it were dozens of huge cargo containers, each the size of a semi trailer, with smaller wooden crates and black metal drums stacked between them. All of it was waiting to be loaded onto the ship tied up at the dock. Her heart sank. If George was stuck in one of those containers, how would they ever find her even with police help?

"I'll put down at the end of the building, by the main door," the pilot said, expertly handling the controls. The helicopter banked, hovered briefly over the dock, and then touched down with a gentle thump.

Nancy looked at the pilot. "You're going to wait for us, aren't you?"

The man nodded and began turning off switches over his head, cutting the engine. "I'll stay right here," he said. "That way, I'll be ready to go when you get back." He gave Nancy and Ned a curious look. "What's going on, anyway?" he asked. "Ms. Amberton wouldn't tell me a thing."

"We'll explain everything when we get back," Nancy promised, opening the door and jumping down onto the pavement. It felt very

116

solid under her feet after the ride. "Ready, Ned?"

"As ready as I'll ever be," Ned answered.

"Come on," Nancy said. "We'll find her."

Although the security floodlights on the building weren't bright, Nancy could see the outlines of a twenty-foot door in the end of the metal building. It was big enough to drive a freight train through. Beside it, there was a smaller door. Over it hung a sign: "Authorized Personnel Only. Guard Dogs On Patrol."

Nancy shuddered. "Guard dogs," she whispered. "I don't like the sound of that."

"We're authorized personnel," Ned reminded her as she put the key carefully into the lock.

"The dogs don't know that," Nancy said grimly. "I suppose Ms. Amberton called to alert any guards on duty. Maybe they'll help us."

Inside, the lights were even dimmer than the ones outside. Most of the vast space was in mysterious shadow. As Nancy's eyes got accustomed to the dark, she was able to make out a long center aisle. It ran the full length of the building. The rest of the warehouse was stacked with containers and crates.

"Now that we're in here, where do we start?" Ned wondered out loud. His voice was almost lost in the enormous silence. "Maybe we ought to yell. If George hears us—"

"George will be bound and gagged," Nancy pointed out. "Let's split up. We'll cover more ground that way."

"Not on your life," Ned objected. "I don't want to have to search for *both* of you in here. This place is so big that we should have a compass and a map just to find our way around." He frowned and stuck his hands in the pockets of his pants. "Besides, how do we even know she's here."

"Somehow I'm sure of it," Nancy replied. "You were right this afternoon when you said you thought George was being held in the wharf area." She pulled out her flashlight. "But there's something I don't understand. I mean, why would the kidnapper let us walk in and just pick her up? Do you suppose—"

"Look," Ned interrupted, "it's nearly seven-thirty. Let's find George first, *then* we can worry about the kidnapper."

"Right," Nancy said, flicking on her flashlight. "I wonder where the police are, though." She shined it at the huge, trucklike containers that were parked along the wall. "Most of these containers are sealed. They may have been here waiting for a ship for months. If we assume that George is still alive and the kidnapper wants to keep her that way—at least for the moment—it stands to reason that she's probably not sealed in one of these. Let's start checking all the loose crates."

With Ned behind her, Nancy started down the long center aisle. It was like walking down a narrow canyon between two mountains.

"My guess is that the crate we're looking for won't be nailed shut," Nancy went on. "The kidnapper would need to get at her in a hurry."

Nancy's small flashlight barely lit up the first group of wooden crates, but it appeared that they were all nailed solidly shut. Between the cracks of the crates Nancy could see the glint of polished steel. The crates must be full of heavy equipment. There were black letters stenciled on the side.

"What does it say?" Ned asked.

"It's French for 'This Side Up,'" Nancy replied, stepping backward. Suddenly the silence was broken by a piercing squeal. Nancy saw a huge black shape dart along the top of one of the crates and disappear behind it.

Instinctively, she pressed against Ned. "What was that?" she asked breathlessly.

"It's just a rat," Ned said reassuringly.

"Just a rat?" Nancy hissed. "Did you see the *size* of that thing? It was as big as a cat!"

"Come on," Ned said. "It doesn't look like there's anything back there."

"Wait!" Nancy said, grabbing the sleeve of his sweater. "What's that rat doing here?"

Ned frowned. "This place must be full of them," he replied. "Warehouses always are."

"Maybe, but most of this stuff is heavy machinery, Ned. Rats can't eat cold steel."

"Maybe not, but if George is here, she's got to have food," Ned exclaimed. "The smell of the food could have attracted the rats."

Nancy flicked her light over the ten-foot-high stack of crates. "Look!" she exclaimed. "Look at that!"

Behind the stack, along the wall, was a large black chemical drum marked Toxic Waste.

"What do you suppose *that* stuff is doing here?" Ned asked. "It doesn't fit in with the rest of this cargo."

"Let's take a look at it," Nancy said. Together, they climbed over a half dozen crates to get to the mysterious black drum.

"Hey, this is really weird," Ned said, examining the drum. "It's got holes in the top. Who'd punch holes in a barrel of chemicals?"

"Air holes!" Nancy cried.

She leaned down, listening. A dull moan sounded from inside the drum.

"George! It's George!" Nancy exclaimed. "How do we get her out?"

"I think we can pry the lid off," Ned said. "It's pressed on like the top of an orange juice can."

"Look, there's a crowbar," Nancy said, reaching for a heavy tool that was leaning against a crate. "I'll bet that's what the kidnapper's been using to open the drum."

Nancy handed the crowbar to Ned, who began to pry the lid loose. Finally it popped off and crashed to the cement floor with a loud clang that echoed eerily down the length of the warehouse.

Nancy shined her flashlight down into the drum. George was there, hands bound tightly behind her, a dirty gag in her mouth. At her feet were the remains of a half-eaten sandwich. She was still wearing the shorts and running shirt she'd been wearing when she was kidnapped.

"Quick," Nancy said. "Let's get her out of here! The guards probably heard the noise."

Ned pulled George out. Her eyes were half-closed as she slumped against him.

Nancy pulled out the gag. "George!" she whispered urgently. "George, are you all right?"

Groggily George opened her eyes and managed a nod. She closed her eyes again, and it looked as if she'd fainted.

"My guess is that she's doped up," Ned said, untying her hands. "She can't even stand."

"She's shivering." Nancy pulled off her sweater and pushed George's arms into it. "Come on. We've got to get her out of here!"

Suddenly along the wall overhead a little to their right, a light flickered on in an office window. Then another light came on, this time on the catwalk that crossed the center of the building about twenty feet up. A door opened, and somebody came out onto the catwalk.

"Ss-sh-sh," Nancy said, crouching into the shadows. "It must be a guard." Beside her, Ned made sure George was hunched down, too. "I wonder if Ms. Amberton thought to call them and tell them we're here."

The silence was eerie. Then Nancy heard two loud, distinct *chinks*, like pieces of metal coming together.

Ned put his hand on her arm. "That sounded like somebody loading a gun," he whispered.

Cautiously Nancy raised her head over the drum to see what was happening. The silence was broken by a loud *Ka-boom!* A bullet thudded into the wooden crate beside her. Someone was shooting at them!

Chapter

Fifteen

"HEY, WHAT'S GOING on up there, Pete?" The startled shout came from the far end of the warehouse.

"There must be *two* guards," Nancy whispered to Ned. George let out a faint moan.

"I thought I heard something, Charlie!" the guard on the catwalk yelled back. "I was just trying to scare 'em out into the open."

"Do you see anything now?"

The guard craned his neck to look around. "No," he admitted. "But I did *hear* something. Sounded like a piece of metal rolling around on the floor."

"I'll bring the dog down and we can check it out." A door slammed and there was silence.

George moaned again. She was propped weakly against Ned's shoulder.

"Listen," Ned whispered, "with George in this condition, we're no match for a dog. Why don't we just tell them who we are and why we're here? They could call Ms. Amberton to confirm that it's okay."

"No way," Nancy retorted. "They might be working with the kidnapper. You take George and sneak to the exit. I'll cover you guys by getting the guards' and the dog's attention."

"That's too dangerous," Ned objected. "Let's think of something else."

Another door slammed. A dog began to bark loudly. "Go get them, Spike!" the man yelled.

"There's no time to argue," Nancy said, jumping to her feet. "Get going!"

As Ned grabbed George and started toward the exit, Nancy dashed out into the center aisle. She ran down it until she was sure she had been spotted. Then she ducked behind another pile of crates.

"Hey, it's a girl!" shouted Pete, the first guard. "There she goes!" Quickly, he climbed down a ladder from the catwalk. "She's heading your way, Charlie! We've got her between us!"

Good, Nancy thought. It was just what she wanted. With Pete down from the catwalk and coming in her direction, Ned and George would be able to slip past him and out the door at the end. Gingerly, she began to work her way among the crates toward the outside wall.

But once she was against the wall, Nancy realized that she was in trouble. Where were the police? Pete was coming from one direction, with his gun; Charlie was coming from the other, with Spike. Ned and George must be safely outside by now, but *she* was trapped!

"All right, little lady!" Charlie yelled. "We've got you. Come on out now."

Frantically, Nancy looked around. She noticed a large pile of wood shavings that were probably used for packing material. She reached in the pocket of her skirt. Yes, luckily they were still there—the book of matches she had picked up at the Greek restaurant a few nights before.

Working fast, Nancy pushed a large pile of shavings up against the sheet-metal wall. She added an oily sack that had been draped over a barrel. Then she bent over and struck a match to the pile. There on the cement floor, the fire would do no real damage. But if her scheme worked, it would distract the guards long enough to let her get away.

The yellow flames began to spread through the shavings. Seconds later the entire pile was blazing, eerie shadows flickering against the ceiling. A cloud of black, oily smoke spewed out of the flames as the sack caught fire.

"Fire!" Pete yelled frantically. "She must be trying to burn the place down!"

"Forget the girl! Get a fire extinguisher!" Charlie yelled back. "Let the dog take care of her! He'll never let her get away!"

Spike began to bark—short, vicious yips that made the hair prickle on the back of Nancy's neck. The dog sounded as if he meant business. Could she get past him?

Silently, Nancy edged along the wall, behind the crates. She was careful not to make any noise that might attract the dog's attention. Halfway to the door she saw that the two guards were totally preoccupied with fighting the fire. Maybe she was close enough to make a run for it. Cautiously, she stepped into the center aisle.

But there was another loud bark. She threw a quick look back over her shoulder. A large black form about waist high emerged from the shadows. It charged after her with incredible speed, its teeth bared. It was a police dog, the largest one she had ever seen. And she'd never get to the door before *it* got to her!

Nancy dived behind several cardboard boxes and crates, pulling three or four down around her. The dog stopped and glared at her with slits for eyes, growling low in his throat. There was nothing between her and the dog but a half dozen flimsy boxes. Would they hold him back? The dog bared his teeth and growled again, the hair rising along his neck. Still it didn't move toward her as long as she stayed perfectly still. Spike must be trained, she thought as she watched him, to corner people until his master arrived.

Nancy took a deep breath. The palms of her hands were clammy with sweat. She was safe from the dog as long as she didn't move—for a few moments at least, until the guards put the fire out. But if she tried to make a break, the dog would attack her for sure. And from the looks of those sharp teeth, she'd be cut to ribbons in minutes. What could she do?

Just as Nancy was beginning to feel truly frightened, the silence was broken by the hum of a large electric motor. From overhead came the creaking sound of something. It sounded like a piece of machinery moving along a rail.

Nancy looked up. Above her, she could see a heavy rail suspended, like the track for a monorail train. It ran the full length of the center aisle, all the way down to the huge double doors at the end. Attached to the rail was what looked like a small cab. In the dim light, Nancy could still see that Ned was inside the cab. And from the bottom of the cab swung a large hook. Ned had come to rescue her!

"Hey, what's that?" one of the guards shouted. Spike bared his teeth and began to growl again.

127

"It's the crane!" the other one yelled. "Come on! We've got to cut the power!"

Nancy fixed her eyes on the hook as it swung down the aisle toward her about four feet above her head. Could she reach it? She pushed over a wooden crate and stood up on it. The hook was coming within reach now, and she grabbed it—just as Spike lunged toward her. To her relief, the hook began to pull her up out of the dog's reach, until she dangled just above his head. And Ned was taking them straight for the door!

Shouting loudly, the guards were running down the center aisle. They were too far away to get off an accurate shot, but the crane also seemed to be moving incredibly slowly. Then Nancy turned to see the huge double doors just ahead! They were closed tight. She and Ned were going to crash into the doors!

Then a warning horn began to blare loudly. Slowly, just as the crane reached the opening, the enormous doors slid open, just wide enough for the crane to pass through. A blast of cold, wet night wind hit Nancy in the face, nearly taking her breath away. The rush of air came from the helicopter, which was hovering noisily just outside the building. Its landing lights were on, and its marker beacon flashed bright against the darkness. It was raining lightly.

"What in the world is that!" Nancy heard

one of the astonished guards shout. She saw them duck behind one of the containers.

"Nancy! Get in the helicopter!" Ned shouted as he slid down the ladder from the cabin of the crane. "I'll take care of the dog!"

Nancy let go of the hook and dropped to the ground with a thump. As she raced toward safety, Ned wrapped his jacket around his arm, holding it bent in front of him like a shield. Crouching low, he ran straight at Spike.

"Look out, Ned!" Nancy yelled. She ran toward the helicopter, hovering three feet above the dock, and hoisted herself into the copilot's seat. George was slumped in a backseat, breathing in great gulps.

Growling ferociously, the dog charged Ned. It sunk its teeth into the jacket he had wrapped around his arm. Stubbornly, the dog held on as Ned began to back toward the helicopter, dragging the fighting dog with him.

One of the guards ran to the open door. "Stop!" he shouted. "Stop or I'll shoot!"

"No!" the other one yelled. "It's a company helicopter! Don't shoot!"

"Hold on, kids," the pilot commanded. "We're getting out of here!"

"Wait for Ned!" Nancy shrieked as the pilot began to rev up the engine. The helicopter rose another couple of feet.

As the copter began to rise higher, Ned lunged for it and hooked his free arm over the landing skid. Just as his feet were dragged free of the ground, he straightened out his other arm. His jacket peeled off his arm, and the dog dropped with a splashy thud into a puddle on the dock below. Ned crawled over the skid and into the backseat of the helicopter as the dumbfounded guards stared at him, their pistols hanging at their sides.

Leaning over the back of the front seat, Nancy cheered and flung her arms around Ned. "Oh, Ned!" she cried. "You're safe!"

"Are *you* all right?" Ned asked anxiously, gently brushing her cheek with his hand.

Nancy kissed him quickly. "I'm fine," she said. "What about George?"

George looked up, dazed. "Where are we?" she asked. "What happened?"

"We're on our way back to the Cherbourg Building," Ned told her, pointing to the lights on the rain-slicked streets below. The wiper blades on the helicopter made a comfortable *thunk thunk.* "You're safe now."

Nancy looked at George. "Did you see the person who kidnapped you?" she asked eagerly.

George frowned. "No, I didn't see her," she said slowly. "But I—"

"Her?" Ned broke in.

George nodded, looking pleased with herself. "I couldn't see her face, but it was a woman. I'm sure of it. I could tell by her voice." She grinned. "I got even, too—at least a little," she added smugly. "I bit her, right on the hand."

"You *bit* her," Nancy repeated, in a wondering tone. Something was nagging at the back of her mind, but she still wasn't sure what it was.

"Yes," George said, "she came to bring me something to eat, and when she took the gag out of my mouth, I—"

But George didn't get to finish her sentence. The helicopter engine had begun to sound funny, as if it had to work harder to keep going. Then, suddenly, there was just silence —a terrifying silence.

George grabbed Ned's arm. "What's going on?" she cried.

"Engine failure," the pilot said tersely, snapping switches on the control panel in front of him.

Nancy stared at the panel. The gauges were all falling toward zero—all except the altimeter. It was spinning counterclockwise, faster and faster. Nancy's stomach felt the way it did in an elevator, when it went down too fast. And then from behind her, she heard George's thin, high-pitched scream.

"We're going to crash! We're all going to die!"

Chapter

Sixteen

We've got to find a clear spot to put down—and fast," the pilot told Nancy. "I'm going to have my hands full. Get on the radio!"

Nancy looked at the radio doubtfully. "How does it work?" she asked.

"Pick up the mike. When you want to talk, press the button on the side. I'll tell you what to say."

Nancy picked up the large black microphone clipped to the instrument panel, the flexible cord dangling beneath it.

"Now, press the button and say, 'Mayday, Mayday. This is Bell Whiskey Seven Seven One Zero Three Alpha. Over,'" the pilot directed. The copter lurched to the left and he righted it, but with difficulty.

Nancy pressed the button and blurted out, "Mayday! Mayday! This is Bell Whiskey Seven Seven One Zero Three Alpha. Over."

"Now let go of the button," the pilot commanded. "They can't answer while you're on the air."

There was a long silence. Nancy wondered if anyone had heard them. Then she heard a crackle of static and a calm voice came through.

"Roger, Seven Seven One Zero Three Alpha. This is Montreal Air Traffic Control Center. What is the nature of your emergency?"

Nancy took a deep breath and tried to keep her voice as calm as the radio voice. "We're having engine failure," she said.

"Roger, Seven Seven One Zero Three Alpha," the voice responded. "What is your location? Can you return to base? Over."

"Negative!" the pilot replied. "We have total engine failure. We're at twelve hundred, descending at seven hundred feet per minute."

"The pilot says we're going in, fast," Nancy said, glancing down. "We're somewhere just north of the river."

"Hey, isn't that City Hall?" Ned asked as he leaned forward, pointing over Nancy's shoulder.

"We're just southwest of City Hall," Nancy added.

"Roger, Seven Seven One Zero Three Alpha. We have you on the screen. Suggest you try an emergency landing in Place Jacques-Cartier. Wind northwest at fifteen, gusting to twenty-five. Emergency equipment is on the way. Good luck."

"Roger, out," responded the pilot.

"Roger, out," Nancy repeated.

"Okay, everybody," the pilot said. "Hang on! I'm going to autorotate!" He began to turn the rotor control.

"What's that?" George gasped.

"He's changing the angle on the rotors," Ned told her. "It'll slow our fall a bit."

As if an invisible hand had lifted them, Nancy felt the copter's descent slowing. But they were already over the plaza, and she could tell that they were still falling too fast. They were going to crash! Feverishly, the pilot began to flip switches. Suddenly the lights went out. The cabin was pitch dark. A second later, with a sickening crunch, the helicopter slammed into the concrete.

There was silence.

"Nan?" Ned asked. "Are you okay?"

Nancy took a deep breath. She was jammed into her seat at a crazy angle, and her blouse was torn where she had caught it on something. But other than that, she was fine.

"I'm okay. What about George?" she asked,

unbuckling her seat belt. Beside her, the pilot was struggling to get his door open.

"I'm still alive," George said in a dazed voice. "I can't believe it, but I'm still alive!"

Nancy pushed the door open and jumped out onto the pavement. The force of the impact had crushed one of the skids and the copter was tilted over. The tip of one rotor had ripped through a bed of pansies, scattering wet flowers all over the sidewalk.

"Everybody out!" the pilot shouted. "This thing could blow sky-high any second!"

Working quickly, Nancy helped Ned pull George out and take her to a nearby bench. Fire trucks, their sirens wailing, pulled up at the curb. Police cars were right behind them.

Nancy turned to the pilot. "Can we find out what happened to the engine?"

"Not now. I wouldn't want to risk being near it if it blows up," the pilot said cautiously.

"But if it goes up, we'll *never* know," Nancy pointed out. "And I have the feeling that this is important."

Nancy and the pilot ran to the rear of the helicopter. Something black and gooey was oozing out from under it.

"Looks like an oil problem to me." He took a look at the engine. Black goop was everywhere.

"Incredible!" the pilot exclaimed. He stared uncomprehendingly at the mess. Then he bent over and began to explore underneath the engine with his fingers.

"What is it?" Ned asked, coming up behind Nancy and the pilot.

"Looks like the oil drain plug fell out," he said. "If that happened, the pressure in the system would blow all the oil out in seconds." He wiped his hands on his pants, a puzzled look on his face. "Funny thing, though, the warning light never came on."

Ned disappeared around the helicopter. As she watched him go, Nancy became aware of a new, sharper smell, mixing with the heavy, oily smell of the engine.

"What's that smell?" she asked.

"Aviation gas!" the pilot exclaimed. He grabbed her arm and yanked her away. "The fuel line must've broken. Let's get out of here!"

The fire chief ran up. "We've evacuated the entire area," he said. "Now, you get back, too!"

"Ned!" Nancy yelled, looking around. A tiny blue flame was licking up at the engine compartment. "Ned, where are you!"

Then, to her horror, she saw him. He was on his back on the floor of the cockpit, legs dangling out the door. He was examining something under the instrument panel.

"Ned!" Nancy screamed. "Get out! It's going to explode!"

Ned worked for an instant longer, and then slid out from under the instrument panel and bolted toward them. Behind him, the blue flame suddenly burst into bright yellow and rapidly enveloped the rear of the disabled copter.

It exploded with a tremendous *Bang!* Nancy felt a *whoosh* of superheated air rush over her head, just as Ned crashed into her and they both went down. Above them, large pieces of metal sailed up in a column of yellow flame and thick black smoke.

"Ned?" Nancy pushed Ned's heavy weight off her and sat up. Bits of metal were raining down onto the wet pavement. The helicopter was burning out of control.

"I'm okay," Ned grunted. "Are you?"

"Yes," she said, rubbing her knee where she'd skinned it on the pavement as she fell. "What were you *doing* in the cockpit? One more second and you'd have been killed!"

"I was looking for a broken wire," Ned said grimly. "The wire to the oil warning light."

"Did you find it?"

"Yeah, but it wasn't broken. It was *cut!*"

The pilot came up behind them. "You mean somebody sabotaged us?"

Nancy turned. "Someone must have loosened the drain plug *and* cut the wire."

137

"Right," Ned put in. "And if we'd crashed into the river, nobody could ever have figured out why."

Nancy stared at him. "Ned," she said, "I think I know who it was."

Chapter

Seventeen

NANCY DREW! WHAT are you doing here!"

Nancy turned quickly. It was Annette LeBeau, wearing a raincoat. She had an umbrella in one hand and a microphone in the other. Behind her were two guys with lights and TV cameras, shooting the burning helicopter.

"Annette!" Nancy exclaimed. "What—"

"We heard the police bulletin about the crash," Annette told her. "I was there, so the station manager sent me to cover the crash. We need to get the spot filmed in time for the ten o'clock news." She looked at the burning helicopter. "Hey, isn't that a Cherbourg helicopter?" She looked back at Nancy, comprehension dawning. "Wait, you mean, you—"

Nancy nodded. Then suddenly she got an idea. "Listen, Annette," she said, "I need to ask you a favor."

But Annette wasn't listening. "What a story!" she said excitedly. "'Helicopter crashes in downtown Montreal. Nancy Drew survives!' All the networks will pick this one up." She turned as Ned and George came up. "Are these your friends?"

Nancy nodded. "Yes, this is Ned Nickerson," she said, introducing them. "And George Fayne. George was kidnapped from Olympic Stadium. We were rescuing her when the copter went down."

"Better and better. A rescue effort, a thwarted kidnapping—that'll make the story gold!" She pointed toward the helicopter, where the pilot was talking with police. "Listen, the three of you go stand right over there, with the police in the background. I'll interview you."

"Wait," Nancy said, trying to interrupt. "I have to talk to you."

"After we shoot," Annette replied hurriedly. "Ned, you put your arm around Nancy. We'll play up the romance angle." She gestured to one of the cameramen. "Max! Get the camera over here on the double! We've got survivors to interview! I want as much smoke and flame in the picture as possible. And be sure to get the cops, too."

Nancy grabbed her arm. "Wait!" she cried. "I don't want you to do a story—at least, not this one. Not now!"

Annette frowned at her. "What do you mean, you don't want a story? This is a terrific story! We'll probably make all the American shows tomorrow."

Nancy shook her head violently and pulled Annette over to the side. "Listen," she said, in a low voice, "can you kill the survivor angle?"

Annette nearly dropped her mike. "What do you mean, kill it? You're all alive, aren't you? I mean, everybody walked away from the crash. Right?"

"Right," Nancy said. "But a certain person needs to believe that this was a *fatal* crash —that there were no survivors."

Annette stared at her. "Who? Who needs to believe it?"

"The person who's blackmailing you," Nancy replied soberly. "The same person who kidnapped George and sabotaged the helicopter."

Annette's mouth dropped open. "Am I hearing you correctly?" she asked.

Nancy nodded.

"If I don't mention any survivors, will it help you catch the blackmailer?"

"I can almost guarantee it," Nancy said. "Now, here's what I want you to do."

When Nancy had finished giving instructions, Annette hesitated.

"Well," she said slowly, "I don't like it, but okay. I have no idea how I'm going to explain it to the manager. He won't be happy that we've missed this story."

"If this thing works, you'll have an even bigger story," Nancy told her. "You'll be able to scoop every newspaper and television station in Canada. *And* you'll have the blackmailer off your back."

Reluctantly, Annette nodded. "Okay, I'll do it," she said, looking at her watch. "But you'll have to give me about twenty minutes. It'll take us at least that long to get back to the station and air this."

"Great," Nancy said. "That's just about right." She grinned. "Keep your fingers crossed."

"You bet," Annette said. "Good luck!" She stood up and raised her voice. "Hey, Max! Let's get over to the helicopter. We've got some filming to do if we're going to be on the air at ten."

Max looked at Nancy and her friends. "What about them?" he asked.

"Who?" Annette asked blandly. "Come on, get that camera rolling! Lights? Where are the lights?"

"Okay, gang," Nancy said to George and Ned, "let's get out of here."

"Boy, I'm ready," George said with a sigh. She pulled Nancy's sweater closer around her, shivering. "Hot shower, here I come."

Ned laughed. "I think Nancy has something else in mind," he said.

"Yeah, something like wrapping up a case," Nancy replied. "We promised Ashley Amberton that we'd let her know when we got back so she'd know we're safe. Let's go pay her a visit."

In the taxi Nancy told Ned and George what she had figured out, and what she wanted them to do.

"The important thing here is the timing," she said. "Surprise is absolutely necessary, so it'll all have to run like clockwork."

Ned picked up Nancy's hand and squeezed it. "Don't worry," he assured her. "It will."

"I certainly hope so," George said. She was shivering so hard that her teeth were rattling. "I want to get out of these clothes. I'm freezing! And I must smell like a locker room."

Nancy grinned. "I've got to admit that you *are* pretty ripe," she said. "But what can you expect from somebody who's been living in a barrel?"

She ducked the punch that George aimed at her.

* * *

At the Cherbourg Building, they signed in with the guard at the lobby desk and went up in the elevator. The deserted building was dark and spooky. But when they got to the fifteenth floor, Nancy could see the light at the end of the hall. Ashley Amberton must still be there, working late just as she'd promised.

Quietly, with Ned and George right behind her, Nancy tiptoed down to the end of the hall and pushed open the door to Ms. Amberton's outer office. It was dark and empty, but through the glass window over the secretary's desk, they could see into the inner office. Ms. Amberton was there, sitting behind her desk, signing papers with her bandaged left hand. The door to the outer office hung slightly ajar, and Nancy could hear the *scratch-scratch* of the woman's pen on the paper.

"It's dark in here," Nancy whispered, "so she can't see us." She gave Ned a little push. "Okay, Ned," she said. "Get going. And be careful out there!"

Ned touched her cheek affectionately. "I will. You, too, Nan," he said. "Watch yourself." He disappeared into the darkness.

"What time is it?" George whispered.

Nancy looked at her watch. "Three minutes to ten," she said quietly. "That phone should ring just about *now.*"

As if on cue, the telephone on Ashley Amberton's desk rang. She reached for it.

"Hello," she said curtly. And then, with a little surprise, added, "Oh, hello, Ms. LeBeau." She listened intently for a moment, her lips tightening. "A Cherbourg helicopter?" she asked, a deep note of concern in her voice. "Yes, of course. I'll turn it on right now. Thank you for calling." She put down the phone and picked up the television remote control and flicked it on.

A few minutes later, the news came on. It was the usual scene, Nancy saw—two anchorpeople sitting beside each other, behind a desk. "And now," one of them said, in a deep voice, "we take you to Annette LeBeau, at the scene of the crash. Annette?"

The scene shifted to the dark, rain-swept plaza. In the background was Nelson's Column, and beside it, the blazing wreckage of the helicopter. The camera was focused on Annette LeBeau's somber face as she stood in front of the fire. Behind her were a half dozen firemen and policemen. The pavement around her was strewn with bits of metal.

"Thank you, Carl," Annette said into the microphone. The rain was dripping off the black umbrella she held. "We're at the scene of a tragedy that apparently took four lives in downtown Montreal just moments ago. A Cherbourg Industries helicopter crashed on Place Jacques-Cartier, directly in front of Nelson's Column. Narrowly missing the few evening strollers braving the rain as it lost power and crashed, the helicopter burst into flames almost immediately. First reports are that there were four people on board, but there appear to have been no survivors. We'll get back to you as soon as we have more details." The camera left Annette and zoomed in on an ambulance, parked at the curb. "A terrible tragedy in downtown Montreal," Annette concluded. "And now, back to you, Carl."

Ashley Amberton turned off the television set. Then, as Nancy and George watched from the darkened office, a triumphant smile spread across her face. She reached in her desk and poured herself a drink. Then she took out a file folder and pulled out a newspaper picture of Nancy. She held it over an ashtray on her desk and lit it with a cigarette lighter.

"Ah-ha, Nancy Drew!" she said, gloating as the flame spread across Nancy's face and the paper disintegrated into ash. "Who's the best mind of crime? It's no longer you, Nancy Drew—it's Ashley Amberton, blackmailer, kidnapper, and murderer extraordinaire!" And she lifted the glass in a toast to herself.

Just then Nancy opened the door and stepped into the office.

"Sorry, Ashley," she said calmly. "But it appears that your little plan didn't work so well after all."

Chapter

Eighteen

Nancy? Nancy Drew? But I thought—"
Ashley Amberton stood up behind her desk
and swallowed hard, her face turning a pasty
white. "But the television broadcast just said
that the helicopter crashed! It said that you
were all dead!" She pulled off her glasses,
obviously fighting for control. "I was simply
thunderstruck. How could such a horrible,
horrible thing have happened?"

"It happened," Nancy said calmly, "because
you loosened the oil drain plug and discon-
nected the warning light." She smiled slightly.
"I have to hand it to you, Ashley. You thought
of everything. If the copter had gone down
before we found George, we'd be out of the
way and there'd be plenty of time to get rid of
George. And if it went down with all of us

aboard . . ." She shrugged. "Either way, you'd come out a winner."

"A winner?" Ms. Amberton pulled herself up. "I don't know what you're talking about. Why, I was shocked to hear—"

"It's no use, Ashley," Nancy said, raising her voice. "I know all about it. I know that you blackmailed the Cherbourg employees. It was so easy for you to find out their secrets, wasn't it? You simply poked around in their personnel files, didn't you? And you were also the one who poisoned Monique when you took flowers to her the day before she fell ill. You also stole the notepaper and the liquid nitrogen from Dr. Dandridge's office when you took candy to his staff."

Ms. Amberton smiled. "You have a very lively imagination, my dear," she said smoothly. "No wonder you've made such a name for yourself as a detective. Are you finished yet?"

"No, there's more," Nancy told her. "Much more." She pointed to the charred remains of the newspaper photo in the ashtray. "You made up the phony headline to scare me, and you arranged for the passes to get us into the stadium. And of course, it was you who phoned Jacques Olivier and told him to run us down."

Ms. Amberton frowned. "Me? What makes you think that?"

Nancy smiled. "You knew we'd be at the

plaza, watching Emile Dandridge drop the money into the trash can. Remember? I phoned you and *told* you we were going to be there." She shook her head. "It was so obvious, I don't know why I didn't see it right away. You were the *only* one, besides the doctor, who knew we'd be there. In fact, you were the only person in Montreal who knew every move we made."

"So you've figured it all out," Ms. Amberton asked archly. "What made you suspect me? It wasn't just that I knew where you were or you'd have figured this out right away."

"True. Your question about the damage to the stove when I told you about the liquid nitrogen spill was the first thing. I didn't think about it at the time, though. It was only this evening, when everything began to fall into place, that I remembered our conversation."

"Yes, that was rather an undisciplined remark," Ms. Amberton admitted. "I realized immediately that you hadn't told me *where* in the kitchen the spill had occurred. Was there anything else?"

"Your bandaged hand," Nancy replied. "The hand that George bit. And, of course, the keys. The kidnapper couldn't have gotten into the locked warehouse to hide George—unless *she* had the key, too. Also the police never arrived to help us."

"Well, well, you *are* an amazing young

lady," Ms. Amberton said with a deep chuckle. "I do congratulate you on your stunning detective skills. It appears that you have won this round, doesn't it?"

Nancy stared at her. "So *that's* it," she said. "A game. The whole thing has been a game of wits all along. You've been laying out the clues for me to follow, haven't you?"

"Indeed, yes," Ms. Amberton said, sitting easily on the corner of the desk. "In fact, I think a little boasting is in order, if you don't object. I masterminded the whole thing—all of it. But I didn't do it for the money, of course."

"Of course not," Nancy said, going to the balcony door to look out. "You did it for the *fun* of it, didn't you? It was a test of your abilities—your criminal abilities."

"Exactly." Ashley Amberton beamed. "At first, of course, there was just the pleasure of finding out what I could do, *practicing* in a way. Why else would anyone want to bother with such *insignificant* blackmail victims as poor Monique and Jacques and that miserable Evans girl?"

"But then, as you began to discover your real talents, it occurred to you that there was bigger game out there. So you went after Lake and Annette and Emile Dandridge."

"I knew about their silly little mistakes, of course," Miss Amberton said with a modest shrug. "It's simply amazing how much you can find out if you have an inquiring mind and are determined to learn about people's pasts. But after a while even *that* game lost its challenge. So—"

"So you decided to test yourself against me," Nancy said, looking out into the night. "Even at the risk of getting caught."

Ashley stood up. "Who else is worthy of my efforts? Your reputation, your skill." She smiled a little. "Although I must admit that your friend George *did* tax my physical capabilities to their limit. It's a good thing I've been working out at the gym for the past year. I could never have managed to carry her otherwise."

Her smile deepened into a laugh and she opened the top desk drawer. "As for getting caught, well—you may have won this round, Nancy Drew. But you haven't won the game." She reached into the drawer of her desk and pulled out a gun. Ms. Amberton stepped closer to Nancy, her eyes glittering. "And you're not going to, either."

Nancy's eyes widened at the sight of the gun. "You—you wouldn't," she said in a whisper.

"It's a miracle that you survived the helicopter crash," Ms. Amberton said, her lips taut. "But no miracle can help you escape a fifteen-story fall." She shoved the gun into Nancy's stomach. "Our little game is over, Nancy

Drew, and *I've* won. Now get out on that balcony!"

A loud shout rang through the office as Ned burst in through the balcony doors. Ashley Amberton half turned, her attention distracted, and Nancy aimed a hard, quick karate chop at her extended forearm. With a moan, she dropped the gun and grabbed her arm. Nancy scooped up the gun and pointed it at her.

"It's broken," Ms. Amberton groaned in agony. "You've broken my arm!"

At the same moment, George rushed through the office door with Annette LeBeau, a cameraman, and two burly policemen right behind her.

"You see, Ashley," Nancy remarked pleasantly, "the game's never over until the final move."

While the lights blazed and the camera whirred, the police arrested Ashley Amberton. Her eyes glazed with pain and defeat as they led her out the door. Annette followed close behind, holding a microphone over Ms. Amberton's shoulder and firing rapid questions at her as they went down the hall.

"Whew," Nancy said, collapsing onto the plush sofa. "I'm glad *that's* over!" She looked at Ned. "Thanks for being on time with your cue," she said. "I would have hated to take a swan dive off that balcony."

Ned laughed. "I felt a little queasy at the idea of crawling out that window in the next office and onto a balcony fifteen stories up," he admitted. "But it all worked out."

"And I was a little worried that Annette wouldn't arrive with the police in time for Ms. Amberton's confession," George said. "But we heard every word of it. And Annette had the mike going, too, so I'm sure it's on tape." She laughed. "Annette has even thought of a title for her story," she said.

"Really?" Ned asked curiously. "What is it?"

"She's calling it 'The Other Side of Evil.'" George told him.

Nancy stretched. "Hey, that's a neat title. And I'm glad she got the story. Maybe it'll help make up for some of the misery she's been through." She stretched and yawned. "Well, I guess we can wrap this one up, gang."

"Yeah," George said. "Speaking of a wrap-up"—she hugged herself—"do you suppose we could go back to the apartment—*now?* These running shorts are a little drafty. Besides, I'm dying for something to eat. Something like a sixteen-ounce steak and a bushel of french fries."

"Tell you what," Ned said, pulling Nancy off the sofa and putting his arm around her, "after George gets changed, I'll treat both you girls to a midnight snack. How about it?"

"Sounds super," Nancy agreed. She looked at the pile of ash that was all that was left of the picture Ashley Amberton had burned. "'The Other Side of Evil,' huh? Well, I think we can close this case, for *good.*"

"*Oui,*" Ned and George said together and then laughed.